She hated attorneys, and her supposedly fairy godmothers were trying to hook her up with one?

A small ball of fire erupted from the stove's burners and ignited the paper bag sitting on top.

"Fire," Blossom wailed, running from the room.

"Where's the fire extinguisher?" Glory shouted, frantically pawing through a pile of stuff on the counter. "Someone call 911."

"911!" Blossom shouted.

"On the phone, Blossom. Call 911 on the phone." Glory snagged the small fire extinguisher and ran back to the counter as she pointed the hose. Nothing happened. "How the hell—"

"Here let me," a male voice said, taking the extinguisher from Glory's hands and removing a little peg from the trigger. He deftly pointed the hose and extinguished the bag and its contents within moments. Her *fireman* turned, and Glory caught her first glimpse of him.

"Thank you," she managed, pleased any words escaped her rather constricted throat. Her rescuer wasn't just handsome. He was a hunk—a bone-rattling, heart-stopping, pulse-racing, palms-sweating hunk. Dark hair perfectly styled, a suit that had never known a rack, and a smile that probably had women falling all over themselves to do his bidding were just the beginnings of his hunkiness.

"You're welcome. I hope you weren't experimenting with dishes you plan to serve." The gleam in his dark eyes told her he was kidding. "I was looking forward to having the restaurant open. It will be convenient to work."

"You're an attorney?"

"Last time I checked." He shot her another thousand watt smile, but this time it did nothing for Glory. She knew that, first and foremost, attorneys were actors able to slap a smile in place as easily as other people slapped a fly. Their surface was all gloss and underneath hid a barracuda. Her divorce had been messy—very messy—and she blamed it on both attorneys turning every little decision into a battle, and her attorney-husband who was determined to draw blood.

To Linda Kichline, a woman who believes in fairies and in happily-ever-afters, and whose dedication to the genre and her writers is truly treasured.

Other Books by Holly Fuhrmann

Mad About Max
Magic for Joy

MIRACLES FOR NICK

***

Holly Fuhrmann

MIRACLES FOR NICK

Publisher by ImaJinn Books, a division of ImaJinn

10 9 8 7 6 5 4 3 2 1

ISBN: 1-893896-50-1

PUBLISHER'S NOTE:
This book is a work of fiction. Names, characters, places and incidents are products of the author's imagination or are used fictitiously. Any resemblance to actual events or locales or persons, living or dead, is entirely coincidental.

Books are available at quantity discounts when used to promote products or services. For information please write to: Marketing Division, ImaJinan Books, P.O. Box 162, Hickory Corners, MI 49060-0162, or call toll free 1-877-625-3592.

Cover design by Rickey Mallory

ImaJinn Books, a division of ImaJinn
P.O. Box 162, Hickory Corners, MI 49060-0162
Toll Free: 1-877-625-3592
http://www.imajinnbooks.com

Prologue

"Ooh, la, la, what a handsome man you are, cheri," the winsome blonde whispered in his ear.

Nick Aaronson smiled as he caressed her cheek, reveling in the smooth contrast to his own callused hands. Life didn't get any better than this. "And just think, I'm all yours for tonight...and for as many nights as you want."

"Oh, but Nicky, it's not me you want." The buxom French blonde had vanished, and in her place sat an elderly blonde woman smiling indulgently at him—at least she was smiling until Nick stood up in shock, dumping her from his lap.

"You know, young man, that wasn't very gentlemanly of you." The blonde stood and rubbed her rather well-padded posterior.

"Who are you, and what have you done with Lola?"

"Your dream woman's a fake blonde whose bust is larger than her IQ, and to add insult to injury, her name is Lola? That shows rather a lack of imagination, don't you think, Nicky?"

"Who are you?"

"I'm just a dream. You'll hardly remember me in the morning."

"I don't think I could forget you."

"Funny, most men we've worked with say the same thing." The blonde didn't look very happy at the thought.

"We?" Nick looked around the room, a small French bistro he'd visited about fifteen years before when he and a bunch of college buddies had spent a summer abroad. There was no one in the dream room but him and the blonde.

"Wrongo," came another voice behind him.

Nick turned and saw two more elderly women sitting on the bar, wearing cancan outfits.

"I told you we'd get to wear these again," the redhead said.

"Oh, I'm so glad. I don't know why Gracey finds them so offensive," said a brunette whose clothing was a particularly grassy-shade-of-green.

"Who are you, and what are the three of you doing in my dream? I want Lola back."

"No you don't," said the brunette.

"You just think you do," said the blonde who had joined the other two on the bar and, he noticed, was wearing a cancan outfit similar to the other two except for its banana color.

"What you want is your own-true-love, and we're here to help you find her. We're your fairy godmothers, you see," said the redhead whose red clothing clashed horrendously with her hair. She glanced down at her outfit and sighed. "I know they say redheads should avoid the color red, but I can't help myself. I do adore the color."

"You could let your hair go back to its natural shade," said the blonde.

"Now, Blossom, you know I was born a redhead, and I plan to die a redhead."

"Fairies don't die, Myrtle. And you and I both know your hair was as brown as dirt, just like Fern's."

"Hey, my hair isn't a dirty brown, but yours would be if you didn't bleach it on a monthly basis, Blossom," the woman in green said.

"Why, Fern that's so unkind. I would never mention—"

Nick would never know what Blossom would never mention because the redhead, Myrtle, shouted, "Girls, I've told you time and time again to let me handle the introductions.

The two of you babbling away is enough to confuse anyone."

Confused. Now that word aptly described the way Nick was feeling. This was just a dream—how he knew that he wasn't sure, but he did. And if it was a dream, he should be able to wake up.

Wake up, he commanded himself to no avail. The three strange women still sat on the bar in their cancan outfits, watching him.

"Now, Myrtle, how can you say we're confusing Nick?" the blonde, whose name was obviously Blossom, said.

Fern, the brunette, piped in, "You're arguing just as much as we are."

"Why, I never," Myrtle said.

"That's what you say about dyeing your hair, and we all know that's a lie," Fern said.

"Fairies don't lie," Myrtle practically shouted.

"Except maybe about dyeing their hair," Blossom said, patting her bleached curls.

"Um, ladies, I'm not sure why you're in my dream, but since I don't seem to be able to wake up, maybe you could take your argument elsewhere and bring Lola back? We were just getting to the good part."

"Oh, no you weren't," Myrtle said. "We're here to bring you to the good part, though."

"And what part would that be?" Nick asked.

"The part where you meet your own-true-love and find your happily-ever-after," Myrtle said.

"I don't want love. And I'm happy enough right now—at least I will be if you bring Lola back."

"Sorry, no can do," Blossom said, though she didn't sound the least bit sorry. "Lola's history and Glo—"

Fern nudged the talkative blonde. "Blossom, don't spill the beans."

The blonde looked crestfallen. "Sorry."

"Now, Nick, you'll probably forget most of this by

morning, but we just wanted to drop in and introduce ourselves," Myrtle said. "You'll be seeing a lot of us in the weeks to come."

"In my dreams?"

"Oh, no dear," the blonde started. "You'll see us—"

"Blossom!"

Blossom sighed. "You'll see us when you see us."

"Good night, Nick," the three said in unison.

"Sweet dreams," the redhead, Myrtle, whispered.

Osborn Nicholas Aaronson woke up with a start. What a crazy night. He vaguely remembered three old—well, not old maybe, but certainly no spring chickens—three middle-aged ladies waving at him and dancing on a bar? No, that couldn't be right. He was dreaming about Lola, the woman he'd met when he was twenty in France. Three women such as these wouldn't be a dream, they'd be a nightmare.

Nick put all thoughts of disturbing dream ladies aside and glanced at his clock. He was awake twenty minutes early. Since it was useless to go back to sleep now, he got up. For once he'd get an early start.

***

Anxious to get an early start on the road, Glory Chambers placed her last business suit into the garment bag and zipped it with more gusto than zipping a bag should require.

There. That was it.

She looked around her empty penthouse apartment. She'd saved packing her business suits until last. Maybe it was symbolic. She was packing away her old way of life and getting ready to start a new chapter...a better chapter, she hoped.

Glory Chambers, vice-president of Michaelson's International, a woman with her future charted out to the *Nth* degree, was gone. Taking her place was Glory Chambers, restauranteur. This new Glory was footloose and fancy-free. She was going to learn to relax and take life easy as she built her little restaurant empire.

She was tossing out her antacids and her jumbo bottle of aspirin. Life was going to be good and sweet. The fact she knew absolutely nothing about running a restaurant wasn't going to deter her. She'd been ready to make a change when an aunt she never knew existed bequeathed her the restaurant. Who was she to turn her nose up at fate?

The old Glory might have been inclined to say that fate was only what you made of it, but this new Glory? No, this new Glory was ready to spread her wings and try new things. She might fail, but at least she would have tried.

Once upon a time she thought she'd had the answers to everything in her life. That was until she found her husband in her bed with a blonde named Cynthia whose bra size was probably larger than her IQ. That was the moment she discovered the marriage she thought was forever was over. The moment she discovered the man she thought she knew was a total mystery. That was the moment the old Glory was packed away and the new Glory emerged—this new Glory who was going to take risks and learn to relax.

She picked up the garment bag and took one last look at the penthouse that represented all the things she used to be. Then Glory Chambers turned her back on that old life and marched her blue jean clad legs toward the U-Haul van that was taking her to her brand new life.

One

Glory Chambers surveyed her morning's work as she reached for her umpteenth cup of coffee. Her back might tell her she'd made some progress clearing out debris, but her eyes told her she'd made the merest dent. The Coffee House was still a...she sighed, unable to think of even the slightest kind description for the small restaurant she'd inherited. The truth of the matter was The Coffee House was a wreck.

The small bit of progress she had made was barely noticeable amongst that mess. Booths were unscrewed from the floor and lying on their sides, benches had ripped upholstery, and what serving ware remained whole was covered with a decade of dust and grime.

The attorney who handled her aunt's estate told her it had been eight years that The Coffee House had sat vacant. At the rate she was going, it was going to take Glory at least that long to get it back up and running.

Eight years and probably most of her savings.

Maybe this wasn't such a good idea.

She took another sip of coffee and dangled her feet from the edge of the counter then brushed an unruly curl back from her face and surveyed her kingdom. What a mess.

"What a mess," a voice echoed.

Glory swung around and saw three tiny women standing in the doorway smiling at her expectantly. They were that nondescript age that women reach—not quite ready for retirement, but certainly not just out of college. None of them could be over four and a half feet tall, but it wasn't their size that made them stand out, it was...it was just about everything about them. One had crayon red hair and wore a pantsuit of almost the exact same shade. The one next to her had yellow—not blonde, *yellow*—hair and was wearing a bright yellow dress that flowed loosely over her well-padded body. The third was the tallest and had hair that didn't look as if it came from a bottle. Her worst offense was the puce green wind suit she was wearing.

They were an odd trio, Glory mused. "Sorry. We're closed."

"Of course you are, deary," said the redhead.

"But you won't be for long," added the blonde.

"Not with us around," finished up the brunette.

"I'm sorry, I don't understand."

"We're the answer to your wish," the redhead assured her. "I'm Myrtle, by the way. And these are my sisters, Blossom," the blonde nodded, "and Fern," the brunette followed course. "And we're here for the jobs."

"What jobs?"

"The ones you advertised for."

"I never—"

Myrtle thrust a section of newspaper into Glory's hand and pointed to a circled want ad. "Wanted. A cook, a waitress and a busboy for a new restaurant. See Glory Chambers, proprietor," Glory read slowly. She handed the paper back to the redhead, Myrtle. "I don't know anything about this."

"You are Glory Chambers?" Myrtle asked.

"Yes, but—"

"And this is your restaurant?"

"Sort of, but maybe not for long. I was just thinking it might be wise to simply level this place and put the lot on the market."

"Oh, no, that won't do." The blonde, Blossom, looked on the verge of tears. "After all the time and effort we put into this—"

"You put into this," Myrtle corrected quickly. "After all your work, you can't just give up now."

"Listen, ladies, I've been cleaning for two days and haven't made a dent. And that's just with the dirt and grime. This place needs new wiring, the gas line needs connected, the sink in the kitchen drips and—"

"Little things, and now that we're here, they'll be cleared up in a moment," Fern said.

"Not quite a moment," Myrtle added. "Now, if my two talkative sisters will be quiet and let me finish." The two other women hushed right down, and Myrtle cleared her throat. "Now, Ms. Chambers, my sisters and I would like to apply for the positions advertised in the paper. Fern will be the cook—"

"But, Myrtle." There was a wealth of argument in the brunette's two words.

"—Blossom here will be the dishwasher, assistant cook and busboy," Myrtle continued as if she hadn't heard her sister's protest.

"Bus fair. . . um, buswoman," Blossom said.

"And, you and I, Glory dear, will wait the tables. We'll get red uniforms, of course, to go with our red hair, and—"

"Ladies, I do appreciate the offer, but you see, most of my money is sunk into the restaurant. I can't afford to hire help. I don't know how this could have gotten into the paper. I didn't place the ad."

"Now, don't you worry about ads and money. We'll pitch in cleaning this place up and stick with you the first few weeks you're open. If after that things don't work out, we'll leave without a word. But, I suspect this place is going to be busier than you anticipate, and things are going to work out just right. You've got a prime location, and I'm sure all those courthouse employees will be over all the time."

"That's what I'm afraid of," Glory muttered.

"Pardon?"

"Never mind." Courthouses were full of attorneys, and after the ugly divorce her husband and his attorney had put her through, Glory had pretty much had enough of the entire species. The fact that the restaurant was across the street from whole courtrooms of attorneys definitely was not in its favor.

"Listen, ladies, it's a sweet offer, but the three of you can't afford to put all the time and effort into getting this place running and take a chance of not getting paid."

"Oh, sweetheart, the money isn't why we want to work here," Blossom said.

"We're financially independent," Fern added.

A phrase from a long ago economics class flashed through Glory's mind—*there is no such thing as a free lunch.* She doubted there was any such thing as free employees either. There was always a catch. "Really ladies—"

"You can't afford to say no," Myrtle said.

"But can I afford to say yes?" Glory had a sinking feeling as she watched the three women watching her expectantly.

"What could possibly be wrong with free help?" Fern asked.

"I can think of a few things," Glory said.

Before she could begin a list, Myrtle jumped in. "Let's just play this by ear. We'll pitch in today, and if you don't like our work, you can fire us."

"And if it does work out?"

"Then we'll be back tomorrow."

Something told Glory she was probably going to regret her decision. The old Glory might have shown more caution, but this new Glory decided to throw caution to the wind. She extended her hand to Myrtle, who was obviously the ringleader of the three. "Deal."

***

"Deal," Nick said, standing and shaking hands with the

opposing council. "We appreciate your willingness to settle."

Grudgingly the gray-haired attorney took Nick's hand and shook it. "It wasn't exactly willingness. You had us over a barrel, and you knew it."

"All's fair in love and war."

"And this certainly wasn't love, and last I heard courtrooms weren't exactly war zones."

Nick took no pleasure in winning this particular case, especially when the attorney he was facing was Bill Richards. Bill had offered Nick his first job and had been a close friend since. Disappointing Bill shouldn't have bothered Nick—he was just serving his client's best interest after all, and that was what he was paid to do. But telling himself that did little to make him feel better. "Can you think of a more apt description for them?"

"Halls of justice, heavy emphasis on the *justice,* Nick. Do you really think justice was served here today?"

"Serving my client is what I'm here for. Your client caused him irreparable harm, and seeing him compensated was justice in my book."

"There's not going to be a trial, so you can save your summations. You and I both know that justice was not served here today."

"If you're not happy with our deal, we could still take it in front of a jury."

"Like I said, you had us over a barrel."

Nick watched as Bill walked from the small meeting room. He'd never admit it to Bill, but he didn't feel quite right about how things had worked out, either. But, he was an attorney. His job was to represent his client to the best of his ability. There was nothing that said he had to like his clients, or even approve of their actions, just that he had to do his best.

Bill's client's car had hit Nick's client. Of course, Nick's client had been inebriated, but Bill couldn't prove it. Hell, Nick couldn't prove it, but he knew it and so did everyone else involved in the case. But, Nick's client would walk with a permanent limp because of the accident. And for that he would be compensated—royally compensated. Whether or not he deserved it.

The entire case left Nick feeling like a stereotypical ambulance-chasing attorney. Well, he'd done his best this time, and if it left a bad taste in his mouth, then he'd just have to...

That was just it. Nick didn't know what to do about it. He loved the law, but recently there had been something missing. He wasn't quite sure when it had started—a brief image of old women in cancan outfits flitted through his mind, but he ignored it, just as he planned to ignore the feelings that were plaguing him.

He was an attorney. Not the judge or the jury. His job was simply to serve his client's best interest. That would have to be enough, he sternly warned himself.

But a small voice inside him whispered, as he left the courthouse, "Don't you wish you could recapture your old enthusiasm, that old driving belief that you are making a difference?"

He wished he could have a case that he could really care about and a client he could really believe in.

***

"Believe me, I can handle this," Myrtle—scrunched behind the gigantic old stove with a wrench in her hand and wearing a hot red jumpsuit and—hollered.

"Myrtle, I think we should just wait for the gas man to come back and take care of this." Glory's three new employees had been hard at work all week. They'd scrubbed with enthusiasm...after Glory had showed them the ins and outs of a scrub brush.

Somehow Blossom had restored the booths and benches to almost pristine condition one afternoon while Glory was at the Health Department arranging for an inspection so they could open for business.

They'd all painted the restaurant in bright, primary colors...green, yellow and red, much to Myrtle, Fern and Blossom's delight. Glory had to admit the colors really made a difference in bringing the old diner back to life. They'd kept the Fifties look, since most of the diner already looked like it was out of that era. Thank goodness *retro* was in. Paint and elbow grease had made all the difference.

At the rate they were going they could have the doors open within days.

At least they could if Myrtle didn't blow them up. "Really, Myrtle, let's just wait for the gas man to come back."

"Believe me, I know what I'm doing," Myrtle said, showing no indication of waiting.

"I don't feel good about this," Fern said, backing away from the stove.

"How hard can it be?" Myrtle plunged her hand behind the stove and twisted the little knob on the pipe. "You just turn the gas on and then—"

Blossom rushed breathlessly into the room, a lamp in hand. "Look, this hurricane lamp was in perfect condition I just lit it—"

Whoosh.

A small ball of fire erupted from the stove's burners and ignited the paper bag that had been sitting on top.

"Fire," Blossom wailed, running from the room.

"Where's the fire extinguisher?" Glory shouted, frantically pawing through a pile of stuff on the counter. "Someone call 911."

"911!" Blossom shouted.

"I told you I didn't have a good feeling about this," Fern said, backing toward the door.

"911!" Blossom shouted even louder.

Something in the burning bag gave a small pop, as if it had exploded.

"On the phone, Blossom. Call 911 on the phone."

Glory snagged the small fire extinguisher and ran back to the counter as she pointed the hose. Nothing happened. "How the hell—"

"Glory, we don't approve of swearing," Myrtle said primly from her safely distant corner.

"Here let me," a male voice said, taking the extinguisher from Glory's hands and removing a little peg from the trigger. He deftly pointed the hose and extinguished the bag and its contents within moments. Her *fireman* turned, and Glory caught her first glimpse of him.

"Thank you," she managed, pleased any words escaped her rather constricted throat. Her rescuer wasn't just handsome. He was a hunk—a bone-rattling, heart-stopping, pulse-racing, palms-sweating hunk. Dark hair perfectly styled, a suit that had never known a rack, and a smile that probably had women falling all over themselves to do his bidding were just the beginnings of his hunkiness.

"You're welcome. I hope you weren't experimenting with dishes you plan to serve." The gleam in his dark eyes told her he was kidding. "I was looking forward to having the restaurant open. It will be convenient to work."

"You work around here?" Glory ventured.

"Well, my office is on State Street, but I'm at the courthouse so often that I might as well live here."

Damn. Though she was pretty sure she knew the answer, Glory asked, "You're an attorney?"

"Last time I checked." He shot her another thousand watt smile, but this time it did nothing for Glory. She knew that, first and foremost, attorneys were actors able to slap a smile in place as easily as other people slapped a fly. Their surface was all gloss and underneath hid a barracuda. Her divorce had been messy—very messy—and she blamed it on both attorneys turning every little decision into a battle, and her attorney-husband who was determined to draw blood.

The gorgeous fire-fighting attorney thrust his hand out.

"Nick. Nick Aaronson."

"Glory Chambers." She ignored his extended hand.

"Glory, aren't you going to introduce us?" Myrtle asked.

"Oh, so sorry. Nick, let me introduce Myrtle, Fern and Blossom." Each nodded in turn.

But Nick didn't nod, didn't extend his hand again. Instead, much to Glory's amazement, his face lost all its color, and he looked as if he was going to bolt out the door. He stood staring at her employees as if he was seeing ghosts.

"Nick, are you okay?" Glory asked, concerned despite her animosity toward the entire attorney race.

"Oh, Nicky, maybe you're suffering from smoke inhalation," Myrtle said.

"I could do mouth-to-mouth." Blossom didn't sound as if she'd mind mouthing Nick.

"No," Nick croaked, sounding very much as if he'd mind. "I mean, I'm fine. It's just I've got to go."

"Well, thank you again, Mr. Aaronson," Glory said.

"You're welcome," he shouted as he practically sprinted from the store.

"What an odd man," Glory mused.

"You think so?" Myrtle asked, her tone saying she didn't agree.

"Don't you?" Glory asked her three employees.

"I thought he was cute," Fern said with a sigh. "And brave. Look at the way he charged in and saved our lives. Why, he didn't even ask for a reward. Any descent hero would have at least asked for a kiss for a reward."

"He didn't even want mouth-to-mouth." Blossom looked disappointed.

"Well, he's gone." Glory didn't add, *thank goodness,* but she certainly thought it. She didn't need any attractive attorneys hanging around. She'd had enough of attorneys in the last year to last her a lifetime.

It was too bad that Nick had chosen this particular

profession, because Fern was right. He was cute. And brave. Glory shook her head. No, she wasn't going to give her cute fire-fighting attorney another thought. Right now she had to concentrate on getting her business off the ground.

Trying to sound as if cute attorneys were the last thing on her mind, Glory said, "Now that the fire's out let's go back to work."

"I'll just see about the stove," Myrtle offered.

"No," Glory practically shouted.

When the small redhead's face fell, Glory regretted being so abrupt. Oh, not bad enough to let Myrtle work on the stove, but bad enough to try to salve her feelings. "Maybe you could...um, go see about the sign outside. I thought we should probably spruce up the paint."

"Let's just toss the sign," Myrtle said, visibly brightening. "The place needs a classier name than The Coffee House."

"How 'bout Glory's?" Fern suggested.

"Or The Courthouse Restaurant?" Blossom said.

"The Courthouse—it makes sense to play on that," Myrtle, ever the boss, mused. "How about The Judge's Chamber."

"No, no, better yet, how about Glory's Chambers," Blossom said.

Glory tried to rein in her three employees, though a week's experience had taught her that they didn't rein easily. "I don't think—"

"It's perfect," Myrtle pronounced, as if that was that. "Glory's Chambers. It plays on your name and the fact we're located right across from the courthouse and a bunch of judges' chambers. They might run things over there, but you run things here."

Glory credited her former corporate life with her ability to keep a straight face. *She was the boss?* Certainly no one ever told Myrtle that.

"Glory's Chambers it is," her other two employees agreed.

Glory was outnumbered. It looked as if she was the owner

of a restaurant named Glory's Chambers.

***

Nick Aaronson was a logical man. He stood in a long courthouse hall and stared out the window across the street at the small restaurant. What had happened there earlier this afternoon wasn't logical in the least. It was plain crazy.

He believed in what he could see, what he could touch. He did not believe that dreams came true.

Until today.

He'd met those three women before. Oh, not the redheaded owner—he would have enjoyed meeting her. But the other three. Yes, he'd met them in his dreams. And that didn't make an ounce of sense.

Sure, he dreamed about Lola, a woman he'd met in his teens, but he'd met her and then dreamed about her. She'd been one of the most passionate women he'd ever met—passionate enough that he'd dreamed about her more than once since their brief fling.

That made sense. It didn't make sense to dream about someone, or rather someones, and then meet them.

No, that didn't make sense at all.

Maybe the pressure of work was getting to him. That was certainly a plausible explanation. This last case had produced more than a little stress. Nick liked feeling like the good guy—protector of the weak, defender of the innocent. His client had been neither weak nor innocent. Defending him was a mistake. Nick wished he had never taken the case. He tried to choose his clients with care, but this time he hadn't exercised enough caution.

Seeing Bill Richard's disappointment hadn't helped his anxiety.

Stress. That's what it was.

He hadn't dreamed the women he just met. He simply imagined he had because he was so stressed.

His cell phone rang, and he plucked it out of his pocket

and flipped it open without even thinking.

"Hello?" he said absently, still staring at the restaurant.

"Nick. Do I have good news for you." Good news, at least when it was coming from his mother, was never good and always involved a woman...a woman she was hoping would be the perfect match for him.

"Mother, the last time you had good news, I had to get a restraining order."

"But . . ."

Finding a woman for him had become a bit of an obsession for his mother. He was outnumbered since his two siblings had married and started producing grandchildren. He couldn't compete.

Truth of the matter was he didn't want to compete, not that his wants mattered. Oh, his mother wanted him to be happy, but she couldn't believe he could be happy without a wife.

She was wrong.

His mother chattered merrily on the phone, totally ignoring his lack of enthusiasm. "Oh, Nick you'll just love her. Grace says she can speak three languages. Think how handy that could be."

He turned from the window and walked down the hall, juggled the cell phone into his other hand and opened the door. "Since I'm not planning any trips abroad, I think I'm pretty safe with just plain old English."

There was an audible sigh on the other end of the phone. "Friday night, Nicky."

"No." Nick stepped outside, closed the door, and inhaled deeply. Erie's autumn weather had arrived, and the crisp air helped wipe away the stench of his day.

"Nick, how many favors do I ask for?"

"Well, there was the stewardess last month. She invited me to join the Mile High Club, by the way."

Realizing he'd been standing and just staring at the

restaurant for far too long, he walked down the marble stairs. "Or how about Serenity, who was anything but serene. Or Nancy's friend, Helen's daughter, or Bertha—who used to be a Bert before that little operation...Shall I go on?"

"But maybe Francine is different," his mother offered.

Miriam Aaronson liked to pretend she was tough. She claimed she never cried at movies, and she had a black belt which she proudly displayed whenever she could. But the truth her entire family had realized years ago was that Miriam was a closet romantic who believed in happily-ever-afters. With two of her three children happily married, Nick was her last project. And one other thing about his mother—she was single-minded when she set her mind to anything. Right now, marrying Nick off was her project.

"I can almost guarantee Francine is different and that I'm not interested." There, he'd made himself perfectly clear.

"But, Nick—"

"Mother, I'm quite capable of finding my own dates."

"But I want you to have more than a date. I want you to have what your father and I have, what Max and Joy have found."

"When have I ever fit into a mold, Mother?" He crossed Sixth Street, walking toward Peach Street and the parking ramp where his BMW waited. "Actually, think of it. When have any of us fit into any mold? When the time is right for me to fall in love—if the time is ever right—I'll know it. In the meantime I'll find my own dates."

"If you're sure?" His mother left the sentence hanging a moment, as if she hoped he'd change his mind.

"Positive." He stood directly outside the restaurant that had almost burned earlier. No flames were present now, but a new sign was.

"Glory's Chambers," he muttered. Cute.

"What did you say?" his mother asked.

"Nothing. Not a thing other than no, I don't want a date."

He glanced in the window, but no one was visible. What a relief. He was going to have to find a new parking spot because he planned to avoid Glory's Chambers and his three dream women whenever possible.

"Goodbye, Mom."

"But, Nick—"

"I'll talk to you later." He snapped the phone shut and hurried past the restaurant before anyone inside saw him.

Nick Aaronson's life was perfect, and he didn't need match-making mothers or fairy godmothers from his dreams finding him a happily-ever-after. He was perfectly happy on his own.

He didn't let himself think about his earlier sense of dissatisfaction, or the sense that something was missing in his life. It was just stress. He was perfectly happy.

Two

Glory Chambers was perfectly happy. She couldn't help glancing at the *Open* sign hanging proudly in *Glory's Chambers'* front door. It had only been three weeks ago when she'd walked into a...well, wreck was the kindest word she could think of. And now, like magic, the restaurant was beautiful in a Fifties-retro sort of way. Fonzi, Richie and the entire *Happy Days* gang would be comfortable here.

Glory was working for herself, beginning to build a business of her own. It might not be on the same scope as Michaelson's International, but it was hers...all hers. That is if her three employees didn't start another fire.

But despite the fire, she felt better than she had in years. No antacids, no stock in aspirin. Just healthy and content. She was building a new life for herself, one short order at a time.

"Coffee?" she asked the two women in the booth.

"Sure," the blonde said.

"Are you ready to order?" she asked as she poured.

"No, we're waiting for someone," the pony-tailed brunette said.

"Fine, I'll keep the coffee coming. Just let me know when you're ready." And when the two women did order, Glory would keep her fingers crossed they got something edible to eat. Fern seemed at home behind the grill, but all she'd cooked was breakfast so far. Lunch was a bit harder.

When had she become such a pessimist? Once upon a

time, Glory Chambers had been an almost incurable optimist, but that was before she found Garth in bed with 38 DD Cynthia. Yeah, that was probably the moment her optimism turned to realism, which meant pessimism.

"Now, Glory, what's that face for?" Myrtle asked as Glory swung the door open and walked into the kitchen.

"Just thinking."

"Well, stop thinking whatever you're thinking. It's a gorgeous day, and Glory's Chambers is off to a good start."

"Well, it is going better than I expected," Glory allowed, unable to recapture that initial surge of pride.

"You should expect the best," Myrtle admonished.

"Actually, expecting the worst makes more sense. When things turn out better, you can be pleasantly surprised."

"Glory," Myrtle tsked.

They heard the small bells on the front door chime merrily.

"That's our cue," Glory said, anxious to put an end to the conversation about her newfound pessimism. "Come on, Myrtle. Time you earned your salary. And, by the way, Fern, everyone raved about your pancakes."

"You didn't think I could do it, did you?" Fern asked, amusement tingeing her voice.

"Well . . ." Glory hedged.

"It's okay. You expected the worst, but instead got the best—me. And you got to be pleasantly surprised, right?"

"Right."

"And, just for the record, I want you to know I studied with a French chef for a few months last year, so pancakes weren't a huge challenge."

"I stand corrected. I guess I should have asked about your experience when I hired you." Glory paused. She hadn't asked. She hadn't even had the three small women fill out applications or job histories. That was totally unlike "Cross the *Ts* and dot the *Is* corporate Glory Chambers."

She'd set out to change, and this was just the first example that she was changing. Once upon a time, Glory would never have hired three women off the street, but look how well it had worked out. Okay, it was good if you didn't count almost burning down the kitchen and—

"Don't worry about it, Glory," Myrtle interrupted. "We're just three harmless, middle-aged women who promise that your newfound pessimistic nature will be pleasantly surprised when all is said and done."

"Yes," Blossom sighed. "You're guaranteed to live happily-ever-after."

Glory snorted. "I'll settle for no more kitchen fires and enough customers to keep this place financially afloat. I've given up on happily-ever-afters."

"Lucky for you, we didn't," all three said in unison.

"Come on, Myrtle. We've got customers," Glory said, deciding that ignoring them was the better part of valor.

Myrtle followed her into the dining room. Glory snagged the coffee pot and headed back to her table with the two women to see if they were ready to order. They had been joined by a dark-haired man. He turned his head, and Glory saw it was their *fireman.* "Hi. Nice to see you again. Nick, wasn't it?"

His frown said he wouldn't necessarily use the word *nice* to describe seeing her again. "Yeah, Nick."

Glory felt a flush of embarrassment flood her cheeks as the two women eyed first Nick and then her. Determined to be professional, she pasted a smile on her face, although it felt brittle. "Are you ready to order?"

"I'll just take some of that coffee. I have to get back to work," he muttered.

Glory might not have wanted to be attracted to the dark-haired attorney, but she'd been polite. It was obvious he didn't feel he owed her the same courtesy, which just proved her low opinion of attorneys wasn't far off the mark.

"Fine," she said bruskly.

"Fine," he echoed.

Nick watched Glory try to control her temper, a temper he suspected was as fiery as her hair. He shouldn't have been so short with her, but damn it all, *Glory's Chambers* was the last place in the world he wanted to be. He'd avoided the place like the plague since the fire, not anxious to see his *dream* women again.

The whole situation was ridiculous.

"It's ridiculous, Nick," Joy said, echoing his thoughts.

"Pardon?" He pulled his attention away from Glory and turned to his sister and sister-in-law. When he was dealing with them he needed to be totally focused because they were both as single-minded as his mother. And both had decided his mother was right—he needed a woman.

"I said, it's ridiculous you won't even meet Francine. Grace says she's perfect for you," Joy, his little sister who was a big burr in his backside, repeated.

"That's right. She's intelligent, has a great sense of humor—"

"And a great personality?" he asked sarcastically.

Grace grinned. "Actually, I was going to say she's gorgeous."

"I can have any number of gorgeous, successful women. Why would you think you need to help me find one?"

"Because the women you are choosing are gorgeous and successful and...well, most of them are pretty shallow, Nick," Joy said with a sigh. "I want more than that for you."

"Gorgeous and shallow just happens to be how I like my women. I like going into a relationship knowing that neither of us has archaic romantic notions."

Women like Lola. Yeah, they were the women he fantasized and dreamed about. He didn't dream about women like the three ladies who worked for Glory. No, he'd never dream about women like that.

At that moment her heard Glory say, "Myrtle, look who's

here. Why don't you take this table, since you've done nothing but swoon over your hero since last week."

Nick sighed. A whole week of avoiding the three fantasy women was shot to hell because his mother, his sister and his sister-in-law had to play matchmaker. He was surrounded by interfering women.

"Why, Nicky—" Myrtle stopped short as she stared at Joy and Grace.

"Myrtle?" Joy gasped.

"Myrtle?" Grace echoed. "Why are you here? Is there a problem?"

The small redheaded woman looked nervous. "Well...not exactly."

"You three know each other?" Nick asked.

"You mean you can see her?" Joy countered.

"Or course I can see her. She works here."

"Nick saved my life," Myrtle said.

Grace and Joy both stared at Myrtle, and Nick got the distinct impression that something was wrong...Something was very, very wrong.

"Does he know?" Joy asked at the same time Grace asked, "How can you work here? Doesn't that require that other people see you?"

Myrtle looked even more nervous. "I—"

"Did the three of you suddenly adopt the entire city?" Joy asked.

"Um, Grace, do you remember when Joy was having the baby—how is Zeke, by the way?"

"He's fine. You wouldn't recognize him, he's gotten so big. Why—" Joy stopped. "Oh, no you don't. You're not sidetracking me so easily. What is going on?"

"I want to know why you're here," Grace said.

"Myrtle, you've got other tables," Glory hollered from the other side of the room.

"Sorry. No time to talk now. As you can see I'm busy."

Myrtle turned, clearly anxious to make her escape.

Nick's sense of foreboding was deepening. What the hell was going on?

"Where are Fern and Blossom?" Grace asked.

With obvious reluctance, Myrtle turned around and answered, "They're in the kitchen. Fern's cooking, and Blossom's the busfair. . . person and dishwasher." That said, Myrtle rushed to the other side of the room.

"Myrtle, you're not going to avoid answering these questions," Grace called after her.

"We close at seven," she called over her shoulder. "If you want your questions answered, we'll see you then."

"Is it Nick?" Joy called after her.

"Oh, yes it's Nick. Well, him and—"

"Myrtle!" Glory called again.

"Listen, we'll talk tonight." Myrtle beat a hasty retreat.

"Is what Nick?" Nick hated being talked about as if he wasn't present. But even more than that, he hated the sinking feeling that had plunged his heart into his stomach when Myrtle, Joy and Grace started talking. Something was going on, and he had a feeling he wasn't going to like it.

"You've met Myrtle before?" Grace asked as she toyed with her coffee cup.

"There was a small fire here last week, and I put it out."

"Was she alone?" Joy asked.

"No, Glory and two other older ladies were there." Nick felt as if he was on the witness stand being grilled by some attorney.

"Fern and Blossom, right?" Grace pressed.

"Right," he said slowly. How did they know Fern and Blossom, and Myrtle for that matter?

"Nick, have you ever read my books?" Grace asked.

"Listen, don't change the subject." He knew this tactic, had used it often enough in court. He wasn't about to stand by and let Grace use it on him. "I want to know what's going on, and I want to know now."

"Grace's books are what's going on," Joy said.

"Well, not exactly the books, but the fairies in the books," Grace said. "Or rather the fairies out of the books. It's confusing."

"Listen you two, whatever you're up to, I want no part of. I've got to get back to work. You can fix your friend up with someone else."

"Nick, I don't think you need to worry about Francine anymore. We're done fixing you up," Joy said.

"Oh?" Nick knew he sounded skeptical because he was skeptical. They were done fixing him up? That would be the day. Grace, Joy and his mom had made fixing him up their main avocation in life.

"Yeah," Grace said with what sounded suspiciously like a giggle. "I'd worry more about Myrtle, Fern and Blossom."

"Three old ladies aren't my main concern," he said.

"Who are you calling old?" Myrtle shouted from two tables away. She stalked back over to their table.

"I...I," Nick found himself uncharacteristically stuttering.

"And, don't you two go spilling the beans," Myrtle scolded with a waggle of her finger.

"Myrtle, you have to tell him," Joy said.

"Tell me what?" Nick practically screamed. He hated losing his cool, but the three women staring at him were enough to make anyone angry.

"Tell him, Myrtle, or I will," Grace said. "No one should be blindsided by the three of you. And we both know any explanations you make will be inadequate, but at least Nick will have some warning."

"We're not ready to tell him." There was a plea in Myrtle's voice.

"Tell him, Myrtle, or we'll tell him," Joy echoed Grace's threat.

Nick watched the three women, totally lost. "Tell me what,

damn it!"

"Fine," Myrtle said, sounding very annoyed. "Nick, I'm your fairy godmother." As an afterthought she added, "And don't swear."

"Tell him the rest," Grace pushed.

Myrtle's expression was martyred as she mumbled, "I'm not your only fairy godmother. So are Fern and Blossom."

Nick wasn't sure what the three women were up to—they were probably taking part in one of Max's jokes—but he felt a wave of relief. He could play along with the joke. "I'm such a hard case that I need three fairy godmothers?"

"No. Yes. I mean, yes you are such a hard case—look at all the work Miriam, Joy and I have been through to no avail—but that has nothing to do with your having three fairy godmothers," Grace said. "The fairy council doesn't trust the three of them to go it alone, though I think it might be safer. Each could only do a third of the damage."

"Grace, that's just not fair. We got you and Max together, after all," Myrtle argued.

"You got me kidnapped," Grace said.

Myrtle sighed and set her coffee carafe on the table with a loud thud. "Are you still harping on that?"

"And you got me stuck on a roof, then married to a man who thought I *was comfortable,"* Joy added, her tone suggesting that comfortable wasn't how she wanted her husband to view her.

"Gabriel still thinks you're comfortable. It just took him a while to realize he loved you too."

What on earth were they up to? Nick couldn't figure it out. They didn't honestly think he was going to fall for this, did they?

He tried to resist smiling as he asked, "You're telling me she—"

"—we," Myrtle corrected.

"—that they are my fairy godmothers and that they were

yours, too?"

"That's what we're saying," Joy agreed.

"But what we want to know now is why everyone can see them," Grace said. "I wrote a rule strictly forbidding that anyone but the godchildren could see them."

"You wrote the rules?" Nick's relief was short-lived. It was being replaced by that same sense of dread he'd had a few moments before. This was crazy. No sane human being believed characters from books could come to life, or that their sister-in-law made up the fairy rules. And Nick didn't believe. But he did feel nervous.

Very, very nervous.

"Nick, I can't believe you haven't read Grace's books. She's your sister-in-law after all," Joy scolded.

"But they're romances." There were many things Nick might be open to trying, but reading romances wasn't high on that list...Actually, it wasn't on that list at all. He was pleased Max and Joy had found relationships they were happy with, but that didn't mean he believed in fairy tales, and romance novels were definitely fairy tales. Thinking of fairies made Nick cast Myrtle another glance. What were they up to?

"And real men don't read romances?" Grace seemingly forgot about yelling at Myrtle and switched to Nick instead. "Max reads them."

"He has to. He sleeps with you."

"Nick!" Myrtle gasped. "I don't think that's an appropriate observation."

"I've had enough. I've got work to do. All you matchmakers—mothers, fairy godmothers, sisters and sisters-in-law—can just forget it. I'm perfectly happy with my life." He slid out of the booth and stood. "I don't know what the joke is, but the three of you will have to find the punch line by yourselves because I'm done."

"No you're not," Myrtle said happily. "But you will be."

***

Glory watched Nick storm from the restaurant. What had Myrtle done now? Chasing away customers their first day open for business wasn't the way to build a clientele.

"Myrtle?" she called.

The small redheaded waitress said something to the two women, picked up the coffee carafe and hustled to the counter. "Do you need something?"

"What on earth was that all about?" she asked.

"How would I know?"

"You were standing right there."

"I'm a waitress, not a referee. The three of them were carrying on about blind dates—the women wanted Nick to go on one, and Nick didn't want to go. Can't say as I blame him. He'd have been bored by polyglotal—"

"Polyglotal?"

"Multi-lingual, dear. Anyway, Nick would have been bored with Francine in minutes. She might have an ear for languages, but she doesn't have much gumption. And gumption is something a woman dating Nick Aaronson would need in plenty."

"If this Francine is someone those women were setting Nick up with, how do you know her?"

"You'd be surprised how many things we know." Myrtle studied her a moment. "For instance, I could tell you that they're not all like him."

"All who aren't like whom?" Glory asked. Her three employees often talked in circles, and most of the time Glory felt she was lucky to remain even slightly balanced. At the moment she wasn't feeling very lucky, or very balanced.

"All men aren't like your ex-husband, dear. Some men can see beyond the size of a woman's bra."

"Waitress," a customer called.

"Duty calls," Myrtle said, hurrying away.

Glory stood staring after her, dumbfounded. How on earth did Myrtle know about Garth?

***

Nick stormed down the street. He wasn't sure what was going on, but he was sure that he didn't care. Joy and Grace had obviously decided to call in the heavy artillery, but did they really believe that he'd fall for their fairy story?

Talk about fairy tales. There was no way any sane, rational man would believe that three old ladies were his fairy godmothers. Okay, so maybe he'd dreamed about them before he met them, but that didn't prove anything except his subconscious was trying to warn him that the women were meant to be avoided.

Fairy godmothers? They were just fairy tales mothers told their children.

"Nick, you're such a pessimist."

He whirled and there was Fern, walking right behind him.

"Aren't you supposed to be at work?" he asked.

"You could say that I am working," she said cryptically.

"I thought you were the cook?"

"Oh, Blossom wanted to try her hand at it, and Myrtle did make her my assistant, so I left her in charge for a minute while I snuck out to talk to you."

Reluctantly, Nick stopped. "What did you want to talk about?"

"I know you don't believe in us, but that's okay. We believe in you."

"Fern...right?"

"You remembered. That's a start. I seem to be the most forgettable of us. Maybe it's the hair. I mean, Blossom's is that sunshine yellow, and Myrtle's that bright red." She plucked at a dark brown strand. "Plain old brown."

"I like natural hair better than the kind that comes from the bottle," he found himself saying. Playing the gallant to a supposed fairy wasn't his idea of a good day, but he couldn't seem to help himself. He felt quite rewarded when the brunette grinned.

"So, you do remember that dream. Myrtle wasn't sure you would."

"How did you know about my dream?" That sense of dread he'd experienced in the restaurant was building again in his chest.

"I was there, silly." She studied him a moment. "You still don't believe, do you?"

"Fern, you seem like a very nice lady, but no, I don't believe you're a fairy."

"Not just a fairy—a fairy godmother. There are many types of fairies. And, like I said, you don't have to believe in us. Our believing in you and in your happily-ever-after is enough for now."

"For now?"

"You'll believe soon enough." She turned as if she was heading back to the restaurant, then whirled back around to face him. "And Nick, about that dream?"

"Yes?"

"You can do better than Lola for a dream woman. We all know it, including you. Think about it. You need someone whose brain is bigger than her chest, but more importantly you need someone whose heart is bigger than both."

"And you think a woman like that truly exists?" Nick didn't believe a word of it.

"You just had coffee with two women exactly like that."

"I think you'd be hard-pressed to fix me up with either one. Joy's my sister, and Grace is happily married to my brother."

"Yes, they've both found their happily-ever-afters, thanks to us. So will you." Fern crossed her heart and held up two fingers. "Fairy honor."

"Like I said, I don't believe in you, and I certainly don't believe that kind of love is out there waiting for me."

"Why not, Nick? Your mother and father have that kind of love. Max and Joy have it as well. So why don't you believe it can happen to you?"

Nick hesitated before giving voice to one of his greatest fears. "How on earth can that kind of love happen a fourth time in one family?" He shook his head. "No, it just can't happen."

"You know what your problem is, Nick? You only believe in what you can rationalize. But since you haven't found your soul mate, it's easier to believe she's not out there. But you're wrong. She's out there. In fact, she's right under your nose. She's waiting for you every bit as much as you're waiting for her. And now, thanks to us, the waiting is almost over." Fern turned around and began walking back to the diner.

"We'll see you tomorrow, Nick," she called over her shoulder.

"I don't think so. I think it would be best if I avoid Glory's Chambers." Avoid it? Hell, he was going to treat the place as if it harbored the plague.

He thought her heard her say, "You can't," but wasn't sure.

He stood watching the small woman retreat back into the restaurant. What the hell was going on?

"Nick!" Joy called, racing down the street with Grace right on her heels. "Wait up."

He turned and started walking back down the block. "I think we've all said enough today."

"You're mad," Grace said, practically jogging in order to keep up with his clipped pace.

"Not mad, just disgusted. Did Max put you up to this? He's always had a warped sense of humor."

"If by *this* you mean the fairies, I'm sorry, but no one put us up to it," Joy said. "You know, when I first met the fairies I thought it was Max's idea of a joke as well, but it wasn't."

"So you thought this joke up all by yourselves?" Nick tried to assume his best lawyerly attitude, intimidating and tough. Unfortunately, neither woman looked the least bit intimidated.

"The fairies are no joke, Nick." Grace grabbed his sleeve and forced him to stop his hasty retreat. "Listen, I know you don't believe. I didn't at first myself, and I wrote them. They just popped up in my car one day and announced that they were going to find me my own happily-ever-after. But what I thought I'd found was a one-way ticket to a straightjacket. Then, I got lucky—very, very lucky. I won a makeover that reinvented me. All my jeans disappeared, which wasn't lucky in my opinion, but then I won a new wardrobe, which was. And then there was your brother. I went to see him because I thought I was crazy, but ended up being crazy about him instead."

Nick didn't say a word. He just stared at his sister-in-law.

Grace sighed. "You're right, it sounds insane."

"What's your story?" Nick shot at his sister.

"Did you ever wonder how I ended up in Erie? I mean Ripples was based in Chicago."

Ripples was Joy's non-profit foundation that helped support about a half a dozen different charities.

"The fairies introduced me to Sophie and I fell hard for a lonely little girl. But it didn't take long for me to fall just as hard for her father."

"Did they win you a whole new wardrobe, too?" he asked sarcastically.

"Oh, even worse, they talked me into a marriage-of-convenience with a man I thought loved someone else and who said he thought I was comfortable."

"Gabriel's nuts about you," Nick defended his brother-in-law. That Gabriel was crazy about Joy was evident to anyone with eyes in his head. The two practically radiated love.

"I know that now, but I didn't know it then. I never would have imagined someone like Gabriel could ever fall for someone like me."

"And what's wrong with you? I've always thought you were perfect."

"You, Max and Mom and Dad think so, but that's not what the rest of the world sees. They see a rather plain, average woman. Nothing spectacular. Nothing special enough to attract a man like Gabriel."

"He's the lucky one, kiddo."

"That's what the fairies said, but I didn't believe them. You don't believe them, either, and that's okay. They'll work it out. You'll see. Although there may be times you doubt it will all work out. I know when I was sitting on the roof and listening to Gabriel propose I was pretty sure nothing was ever going to be right."

His sister paused a moment, then added, "But just to give you a little edge, maybe you should pick up a couple of Grace's books."

"For what?" Nick might adore Grace, but reading her romance novels was hardly what he considered a worthwhile use of his time.

"Forewarned is forearmed," Joy said.

"You sound like I'm going into battle."

"Battles are your specialty, Counselor. And I think you're headed into the biggest one of your life," Grace said.

Suddenly, both women broke into laughter.

Nick gave up. There was no talking rationally to two women who didn't possess a rational brain cell between them. He kissed Grace and Joy goodbye and headed back into the courthouse. He wasn't sure what they were up to—and by "they" he lumped together his entire family and his pseudo-fairy godmothers. And he had no rational theory as to why he dreamed about those supposed fairy godmothers before he ever met them, but he wasn't falling for any of it.

Osborn Nicholas Aaronson didn't believe in love, and he certainly didn't believe in fairies. And until someone proved otherwise, he wasn't about to change his opinion.

Three

Wearily, Glory turned the small sign on the door to *Closed.* It hadn't been a bad day—not a bad day at all. The restaurant had had a pretty steady stream of customers, enough so that she had hopes that Glory's Chambers might come close to breaking even this week.

She hadn't been sure about the restaurant's success the day Myrtle blew up the stove, or the day Fern tried to hang up a picture and ended up putting a bowling ball-sized hole in the brand new drywall, or the day Blossom fell off the stepladder and bit her tongue. Blossom's tongue had bled until Fern found a gallon of praline and cream ice cream in the freezer. The freezing confection had done the trick, and the bleeding had stopped.

Of course, Glory could have sworn there hadn't been any ice cream in the freezer, and she'd just cleaned out the huge walk-in unit. But there it was, and they had all shared bowls of praline and cream, one of Glory's favorite flavors.

She was growing accustomed to strange things happening around the small restaurant. Some days she worried that the building was haunted. Things moved while her back was turned. Things she swore they didn't have magically appeared. And then there was the day she'd caught Fern talking to thin air. All three of the women were just different enough that talking to thin air wasn't that odd, but Glory could have sworn she heard the thin air answer back. It had been a soft hissing sort of sound, so she couldn't make out the words, but it had sounded like someone talking.

She hadn't worked up the nerve to ask Fern about it, and doubted she ever would. If the restaurant was haunted, the specter seemed benevolent enough, so she had pretty much decided to leave it be.

Thinking about leaving shook Glory from her reverie. She glanced at her watch. It was way past time for her employees to be off work.

"You three can leave that last load of dishes for me. I've got a few things to do before I head home," she said. "You did a good job today."

Today had been uneventful except for Fern letting Blossom try to make a hamburger that ended up quite burned, and the one table of Myrtle's that had caused quite a little commotion. Thinking about that made Glory realize she'd never gotten a straight answer from Myrtle about what happened with Nick the *fireman.*

The swinging door between the kitchen and dining room flew open and the three ladies, each wearing a uniform in the color they seemed to favor, burst through.

"Myrtle?" Glory picked up a wash rag and started scrubbing down the counter. "About that table?"

"What table? I had a lot of tables today," Myrtle asked innocently.

Much too innocently. The last few weeks had taught her that when one of her employees used that tone something was wrong.

"Your table that was involved in that fight. The one that sent our firefighter rushing from the restaurant. I wanted to know—"

"Gotta go, Glory. The three of us are exhausted. It's been a long time since we put in a day's work like today," Myrtle interrupted.

"We've never put in a day like this," Fern grumbled. "I love to cook, but honestly, all the plebeians want are cheeseburgers. Now, I like a good cheeseburger as much as anyone else, but I made seventy-three today, and that's seventy-two too many. I put a lovely spinach quiche on the special board and sold exactly two slices. I got that recipe from a jinn I met on the Riviera last fall. It's pure magic, and I only sold two."

"Fern!" Myrtle gasped.

"Who did you get the recipe from?" Glory asked, sure that she'd heard wrong. A jinn? Isn't that a genie?

"Jim," Myrtle barked. "She got the recipe from a *man* named Jim."

"Jim?" It had sounded like Fern had said a jinn. What were those three up to now?

"Well, actually it was Jacque, since he was French, but I called him Jim for short," Fern said in a rush.

"Seriously, dear, we've got to go," Myrtle hustled the other two to the door. "Come on, girls."

"Tomorrow by seven-thirty," Glory called.

"Seven-thirty it is," Myrtle promised.

They practically flew through the door. It wasn't until they had disappeared from sight that Glory realized she'd never gotten an answer about Myrtle's table. What on earth had those women said to Nick?

Better yet, who were they to Nick?

With his good looks they were probably part of his harem. Two women battling it out over who got him.

Glory caught herself. No, she wasn't going to think about Nick Aaronson. Oh, she wasn't giving up on men completely. Myrtle was right, not all men were like Garth. Two-timing, boob-infatuated rats.

But even though she didn't plan to swear off men forever, the ink on her divorce decree was barely dry. And she wasn't ready to think about men yet...especially not gorgeous attorney-ish men. No, she wasn't going to think another thought about Nick Aaronson, or any man, for sometime to come.

The bell on the door tinkled merrily. "Hello?"

"We're closed," Glory said as she whipped around. Her mouth dropped open.

Nick.

Maybe she wasn't going to think about him, but she was going to have to deal with him.

"Sorry—Nick, wasn't it?" she asked as innocently as she could manage as soon as she got over the shock of seeing him at her door.

Okay, so she knew his name was Nick. She'd used it enough times after all, but she didn't want him to think she had given him a second thought, and certainly not a third or fourth thought.

"Nick, right." He walked toward her. " Listen, Glory, I want to talk to Myrtle, Fern and . . ."

"Blossom," she supplied.

"Yeah, Blossom. Are they in the back?" He glanced at the kitchen door as if he expected them to burst through it.

"Sorry, I let them go home."

She'd spent the day thinking about Nick's hasty departure from the restaurant. Worrying about why he left was simply concern about business, she assured herself. The fact she couldn't get him off her mind had nothing to do with him as a person...as a man. Not a thing at all.

"Mind telling me what happened today? I mean, you ran out of here like a bat out of hell, and if something Myrtle said or did . . ." she let the sentence trail off, unsure of what she would do if it had been something Myrtle had done.

"It wasn't exactly Myrtle."

"Then what was it exactly? Something those women you were with did?"

"*Those women* were my sister, Joy, and my sister-in-law, Grace. They wanted to fix me up."

"Oh, sorry." Glory had been fixed up in the past, before

her marriage to Garth. And now that she thought about it, Garth had been a blind date as well. "Blind dates are the pits," she said emphatically.

"Thankfully, they gave up on the idea."

"I guess you're a good attorney if you argued them out of setting you up. Women can be pretty insistent about those things." Her friend Bonnie had set her up with Garth, totally ignoring Glory's objections. "It was a good friend that convinced me to date Garth, and that turned out to be a huge mistake."

"Is Garth your boyfriend?"

"My ex-husband."

"Sorry."

Glory wasn't sure if Nick was sorry she had been set up, or sorry she was divorced. "Don't be. He was slime. And if I hadn't listened to my friend and gone out with him, I could have avoided the whole incident. As it was, I wasted five years of my life on someone who didn't deserve even an hour of my time."

"Again, sorry. But then you know how I feel. I mean, I understand Joy, Grace and my mother want the best for me, but they won't allow the possibility that the best for me might be staying single."

Glory was about to agree when she realized she had crossed a line with Nick and they were getting far too personal.

Being personal with Nick wasn't wise, especially since she'd spent the last couple seconds trying to decide just what color his eyes were. They were a dark brown that bordered on black. It was only by concentrating very hard that she could discern the separation of the iris from the pupil.

No, she didn't care what color Nick's eyes actually were, and she didn't really care about his love life—or lack of one—or at least a lack of a meaningful relationship. He could have a series of one night stands, for all that Glory cared, or rather for all that Glory *didn't* care.

"You wanted Myrtle?" she asked, anxious to change the subject and get back to more impersonal topics.

"I had a few questions to ask her."

"Anything I can help you with?"

Nick studied Glory Chambers. For a few moments she'd been warm and engaging, but she'd retreated and was back to her impersonal, all-business mask. He had no problem recognizing the facade, because he so frequently wore a similar one. But it irrationally annoyed him all the same that she felt the need to hide from him.

"Maybe. Could you tell me where she worked before she worked here? Where she's from? Actually any information on all three of your employees would be appreciated."

"I'm sorry. I couldn't release that information without their approval, and besides . . ." she hesitated a moment. "I don't have it."

"What do you mean you don't have it?"

She flushed. And the crimson that tinged her cheeks seemed to emphasize the light sprinkling of freckles on the bridge of her nose. Nick wondered if the sun brought out more, or at least made them more pronounced. He cut off the thought. The last thing he needed to be thinking about right now was a woman. He had enough trouble with the women in his family and his newly inherited "fairy godmothers."

"Well, this is embarrassing to admit," Glory said slowly. "But Myrtle, Fern and Blossom just showed up and, before I knew what had happened, I had hired them. They didn't even care about how much, or rather how little, I could pay."

"And you didn't think that was odd?" he pressed.

"I think pretty much everything about those three is odd. And though the decision to hire them might not have been very business savvy, I don't know what I'd do without them."

"Even though Myrtle tried to burn down the place?" he asked.

"It was an accident," she said quickly, defending her

employees.

"Have there been a lot of other *accidents* like that?"

"Oh, there was a hole in the wall, a couple falls, and a crate of broken dishes—Blossom said she seemed to have a knack for breaking dishes—and quite a number of other problems. But things have gotten accomplished faster than I could have managed on my own. It was like magic."

"Like magic you say?" Magic? Fairy magic? He eyed the redhead suspiciously. Maybe Glory was in on whatever scam his family and their "fairies" was trying to run on him.

"Well, yeah. I mean, I left one night and all the booths and chairs were in pieces. I figured I'd have to replace the lot. Then the next morning I come in and, voila, like magic they're totally reconditioned and looking like new. The girls said they'd gotten so caught up in the work they'd worked the night away, but I can tell you that there was a lot more than one night's work to make these tables look this good. I still haven't figured out how they did it."

Nick pressed the palm of his hand against his temple. His head was aching. It had been aching since Myrtle, Grace and Joy started this whole fairy godmother nonsense. Fern's discussion had intensified it. And what Glory was telling him didn't make him feel a bit better.

"Are you okay?" There was concern in her voice, and for a moment the all-business Glory had receded again.

"I don't think so." This warm, compassionate Glory seemed so at odds with the brusk business-like demeanor she wore like a suit of armor. It was her eyes Nick focused on. Dark blue and radiating compassion. Those eyes drew him in and held him for what seemed like an eternity. "Sorry. It's been a bad day. A bad couple of weeks, actually. A hot shower, a hot meal and a solid night's rest, and I'll be just fine."

"If you're sure?"

He could hear the doubt in her voice. The fact she was

worried about him warmed him, though he wasn't sure why. "Positive."

"I could drive you home," she offered.

"No, that's all right." Nick rose and walked to the door.

"Well, goodnight then," Glory called after him. "You can come talk to the girls yourself tomorrow."

"I just might do that."

Or, if he was smart, he'd simply forget all about Glory's Chambers and everyone who worked there, he thought as the door slammed behind him.

Glory Chambers wasn't the sort of woman a man dated casually and then walked away from. No, she was the kind of woman who would see a couple of dates as the beginning of a relationship. Hell, if Nick wanted a relationship all he'd have to do is turn himself over to his mother, Joy and Grace.

***

"Nick was here last night," Glory said conversationally the next morning as she wiped down a counter in the kitchen. Her strategy was simple. She would question Blossom while Fern was starting the pancake batter and Myrtle was busy out front.

"Nick?" Blossom asked much too innocently.

"Nick." Glory stopped scrubbing the counter and locked gazes with her blonde employee. "You remember Nick, don't you, Blossom. After all, you wanted to do mouth-to-mouth on him."

She flushed. "Oh, *that* Nick."

"Yeah, that Nick. Seems he has some questions."

"About you?" She clapped her hands. "That's great. Once a couple starts asking questions about each other, it's not long until he's asking the question with a capital *Q*."

"What on earth are you talking about?" Glory snapped.

"What Blossom meant was, what did he want to know?" Fern said—batter either done or forgotten—joining the conversation.

"He wanted to know if I had information on the three of you, and I realized I didn't. Not that I would have given it to him if I had, but I should have some information on file."

"What would you like to know about us, Glory?" Fern asked pleasantly.

"Like where did you work before this? Where are you from? Next-of-kin...the normal kind of application questions." She'd ultimately been responsible for hiring and firing thousands of people at Michaelson's. Oh, she hadn't done it directly, but the buck stopped at her desk. So, why was she having such a problem getting information from three older ladies?

"What would those questions tell you that our working here hasn't?" Fern asked. "I can cook. If you have doubts, let me whip up a batch of those pancakes for your breakfast."

Blossom added, "And I can wash dishes—"

"When you're not breaking them," Fern said with a scoff.

"That's not fair." Blossom looked as if she was going to cry.

"But truthful. It's very, very truthful," Fern said. "Anyway, you know that Myrtle can—"

"Myrtle can what?" Myrtle asked as she banged through the swinging door that connected the dining room and kitchen.

"Myrtle can wait," Fern said.

"I don't want to wait, I want you to answer my question." Myrtle looked annoyed, her face flushed to almost the same shade of red as her hair.

"No, you can *wait* on tables, I meant, " Fern hastily amended.

"Of course I can. Any fool can take an order and carry a dinner plate."

"Which is why those tables yesterday got their orders mixed?" Fern asked.

"That was just a small mistake. And my mistakes aren't the point," she said with a glare. "The point is, what are you three talking about? The restaurant opens in five minutes."

"Glory was telling us that Nick came here last night."

Glory had lost control of the conversation and had no idea how it had happened. She was supposed to be grilling Blossom, getting answers and getting to work. Instead, she was being interrogated.

"Nick was here?" Myrtle's entire demeanor changed from annoyed to avidly interested. "What did he want?"

"To talk."

"And he asked questions," Blossom added helpfully.

"Did he ask *the* question?" Myrtle asked.

Fern shook her head. "No, it's too soon. They hardly know each other. He just asked questions about us."

"Oh." Myrtle looked disappointed.

"And Glory realized she didn't have the answers," Fern said.

"Not that she would have given them to Nick," Blossom defended Glory.

"All I was saying was I wanted the three of you to fill out an application!" Glory realized she was shouting. She had never shouted at Michaelson's. She'd always felt that shouting was the sign of someone who didn't have control. She had been right. Here she was shouting, and her entire life was out of control, especially the part that included these three.

"Why apply for jobs we already have?" Myrtle asked.

"But I need some information for the IRS." There. Let them argue that.

"You're not paying us yet, so, there's no reason to bother them."

Damn. "But, if business keeps up, I will be—"

"We'll talk about it then, but right now we have to open." Myrtle clapped her hands. "Come on, girls."

Glory blocked Myrtle's retreat. "Listen, I'm the boss and—"

"Hear that, Myrtle? Glory's the boss." Blossom giggled.

"I *am* the boss!" Glory reiterated.

"Oh, you might be, but Myrtle is always convinced she is," Fern said. "Her bossiness tends to cause problems. Like the time she decided to let April take the rap for a murder, sure that Bruce would save her."

"She keeps saying the fact April almost spent her life in prison was my fault, but we know the truth, don't we Fern?" The brunette nodded her agreement, and Blossom continued, "It was her idea, and since she's the boss, she wouldn't listen to a thing we said."

Glory was totally confused. Bosses? Murder? Life in prison? All she wanted was some information on her employees, like an address and a phone number. Was that too much to ask?

"It's time to open." Myrtle was glaring at all three of them. "Let's go, girls."

Glory watched helplessly as Myrtle marched back into the dining room and Fern and Blossom began to hustle about the kitchen. What was wrong with her? She used to run a multi-million dollar international corporation, and now she couldn't even handle three employees? She was slipping, pure and simple. And Glory realized she didn't have a clue where she was slipping from or, even worse, where she was slipping to.

***

Despite its less than exemplary beginning, the day was going smoothly...too smoothly. That was Glory's thought moments before a tall, model-thin, beautiful brunette walked into the restaurant, spied Myrtle and yelled, "It's you!" in a way that left no doubt in anyone's mind that being *you* was not a good thing...not a good thing at all.

"Now—" Myrtle started to say, but that was all the further she got.

The brunette's shrill scream drowned her out. She stomped a well-heeled foot.

In seconds Glory assessed the screamer. She might have

traded her heels for sneakers, but she recognized Ferragamo when she saw them. And the clothes the shoes coordinated with had never hung on a rack.

"You promised," the stomper screamed. "Two months ago, you popped into my life and promised me my happily-ever-after fairy story. Two months I've waited, like a fool. What kind of mind-trick did you play so that I was the only one who saw you at Bloomingdales and on the plane? Because let me tell you, Myrtle, everyone in this room can see you."

"I'm sorry," Glory said as she rushed forward, hoping to head off a full-scale scene. "Can I help you, Ma'am?"

"Help me? Who are you? Another one of them?"

Glory was sure that the *them* the woman was referring to was her employees, and no, she was definitely not one of them. She shook her head in denial and thrust out her hand. " Glory Chambers. I'm the owner."

"And you let them work for you? You're just as crazy as they are, and for all I know you're in on it too. You're probably a fairy, or at least want me to think you are, but I don't. No, I don't think that at all."

"Honey, you're becoming overwrought," Myrtle said soothingly.

"Overwrought? For two months I've been underwrought, because the objects of my wrought had disappeared. But the ability to disappear isn't unusual, is it? I mean, not if they were fairies. And you promised me a happily-ever-after, but let me assure you Myrtle, this overwrought fairy godchild is not happy. Not happy at all. Where are your two cohorts?"

"Girls!" Myrtle yelled. "You might as well come out and say hi."

The swinging door swung open so fast that Glory had no doubt the two had been lurking behind it listening to the entire confrontation.

"Ma'am," she said, hoping to head off another tirade, "maybe we could take this into the back?"

"You are one of them. You...you lying fairy!"

"I don't know what this is all about," Glory said, "but let's go in the back and see if we can work out whatever your problem is."

The woman laughed then. A brittle, hard sound. "My problem is that I've always been a dreamer. I believed happily-ever-afters were possible. I even believed it was possible that I could have fairy godmothers, and that all the years of loneliness were a mistake—that I was meant to find something more. But, I was a fool. And it's time I woke up and joined the twenty-first century. Fairy tale endings only work in books, and that's where fairy godmothers belong as well. They definitely wouldn't be working in a restaurant."

Blossom moved from the doorway. "We only want to help you. And, we would work in a restaurant if—"

"You wouldn't if you were invisible, which you aren't. It must have been some kind of optical illusion before. As a matter of fact, your entire spiel was an illusion and I'm finally free of your spell."

"Fiona, let's talk," Fern said.

"The only person you'll be talking to is my attorney."

"Your attorney?" Glory asked.

"That's right. I'm suing." With that, Fiona whirled around and slammed out of the restaurant.

An unnatural, weighted silence hung over the dining room.

"That's it, folks. Show's over. Sorry for the inconvenience. Why don't you let us pick up your lunch tabs today," Glory offered in hopes of smoothing over the incident. Today was definitely not going to be a break-even day for Glory's Chambers.

"It will be coming out of your pay," she hissed at the three women.

"You don't pay us yet, remember?" Blossom pointed out.

"I'll think of something," Glory warned. "And the three of you had better be thinking of some answers, because that's just what I want tonight after we close. Answers. Lot's of them."

Myrtle shook her head. "But Glory—"

"Don't *but Glory* me. Myrtle go see to your tables. Ours may be a new version of the boss-employee relationship thing, but I am the boss, and the three of you are going to figure that out tonight."

Glory might be the boss, but she wasn't a fool. Fairy tales and talk of suing made her realize she was out of her league. As distasteful as the option sounded, Glory was calling in a reinforcement—Nick the *fireman,* attorney.

***

"Ladies," Nick said cordially as he walked into the closed restaurant. He slid a chair over to the booth where Myrtle, Fern, Blossom and Glory sat.

"What's he doing here?" Blossom didn't look very happy to see Nick.

"He wanted answers last night, so I thought you could satisfy both our curiosities at the same time." Since he was an attorney, having him present while they discussed potential lawsuits was a good idea, no matter how much Glory wanted to avoid attorneys, especially this attorney. It seemed fate was against her.

Fate, or fairies? a small voice whispered in her head.

No. Glory gave herself a mental shake. She didn't believe in fairies. No matter how strange Myrtle, Fern and Blossom were, they were all too human. And it looked like they might be in trouble. Though she had yet to get a straight answer from them, Glory didn't think they were a danger to anyone except themselves.

"Let's get down to business," she said. She was the boss, and this was just business, she reminded herself.

In unison the three said, "But, Glory—"

"Talk."

"Honey, we're not sure you're going to want to hear this,"

Myrtle said.

"I'm a big girl, I can take it. Now explain what happened today. That woman walked in here and actually screamed when she saw you. Then she proceeded to create a huge scene. So whatever you did to her, it was something big. What did you do? Rob her? Steal her husband? Run over her cat? What?"

"Come on, girls, talk," Nick prompted.

"If you both really want to understand, we've got to start before all this happened today." Myrtle had obviously decided to once again take charge.

"Okay, so start," Glory prompted.

Myrtle sighed, stared into space a moment as if searching for the right words, and then smiled. "Once upon a time—"

"I don't want any fairy tales. Just tell me what happened," Nick snapped.

"Shh," Blossom hissed. "You can't start a story without a once-upon-a-time."

"We don't want a story, we want answers," Glory said.

"If you don't be quiet, you're not getting anything." Myrtle cleared her throat. "Once upon a time there was a writer named Grace. She wrote about love and dreamed of finding it for herself, but she couldn't quite manage it. So, three of her characters broke loose from the bindings of their books and came to her rescue. They found her Max, and now Grace and Max have Charity, a beautiful little girl."

"I'm not buying this, ladies. Glory and I want the truth," Nick said, beating Glory to it.

Why on earth had she ever hired the three? Okay, so she never hired them. They'd answered an ad—an ad she never placed—and said they'd work for free. Glory had just sort have fallen in with them. And now she was falling off the deep end.

"This is your last warning. Another word and we leave." This time Myrtle was the one snapping. "Now, where was I?"

“Max and Grace,” Blossom prompted her.

“Yes. Then after that these three turned their attention to Max’s sister, Joy, who wasn’t very.”

“Very what?” Nick asked.

“Joyful,” Fern answered.

Myrtle glared at all of them. “Stop interrupting. Now Joy lived alone, but longed for more. We found her Gabriel and his daughter Sophie—they needed her as much as she needed them. And now Joy and Gabriel have little Zeke as well.”

“That left just one Aaronson child who needed to find his happiness,” Fern jumped in.

“You?” Glory asked Nick.

“That’s their story,” Nick said with a shrug.

“And we’re sticking to it,” Blossom responded, giggling.

“Blossom, this is a serious matter,” Fern scolded.

“So who do you have in mind for Nick? Not that screaming banshee from this afternoon,” Glory said, shuddering. Not that she was buying into their fairy tale. She might be crazy enough to hire three women off the street with no references or background check, but she wasn’t crazy enough to think they were really fairies. And she didn’t ask because she cared who Nick happily-ever-aftered with, because she didn’t care. No, she asked because...Glory gave up. She had no idea why she had asked, but she did know that she needed to know the answer.

“Oh, no. Fiona’s destined for another.” Blossom clutched her folded hands to her heart and looked practically swoony at the notion. “I know she didn’t put her best foot forward this afternoon, but she’s had a hard life. Never fitting in, feeling like an outsider. But that’s all about to change.”

“We’ve had tough cases in the past, but nothing like Fiona’s.” Fern didn’t look swoony. She looked rather annoyed, as if it was Fiona’s fault her case was tough.

Blossom jumped right back in. “Why you wouldn’t even begin to believe the things we’ve had to do to pull this one off.

Why we—"

"Blossom," both Fern and Myrtle bellowed in unison.

"Now, back to our story," Myrtle said, glaring at Blossom, who blushed and seemed to sink a bit into the booth. "We're here for Nick and his happily-ever-after."

"I'd be happy-ever-after if you all just left me alone," he promised.

"Sorry, Nick. You're stuck with us until you and the love of your life are united."

"I don't want—"

"Who is the love of his life?" Glory asked. Not that she cared. Nick probably deserved what he got. He was an attorney, after all, and—

Glory stopped mid-thought, unsure she'd heard the blonde "fairy" correctly. "What did you say?"

Nick just sat looking thunder-struck as Blossom happily repeated. "You."

"You who?"

"Yohoo? Oh, Glory it sounds like you're yodeling." Fern giggled. "Did I ever tell you about the time I took yodeling lessons from this really foxy gnome named Gunther? It was a couple years—or maybe it was centuries—ago. I always get time mixed up. Anyway—"

"Forget Gunther," Glory snapped. "I want to know what you meant."

"I wish I could forget Gunther but—"

Just when Glory thought she might scream in frustration, Myrtle said with an amazing amount of calmness, "You, Glory Chambers. You're the love of Nick Aaronson's life."

Four

"The love of Nick's life?" In addition to the sense she'd lost her sanity, Glory felt the raw edge of panic building in her chest. "I hardly know the man, and what I do know I don't especially like."

Realizing what she had said, and that the man in question was sitting right across the table, Glory mumbled a hasty, "Sorry, Nick," and then jumped back into her reasons why she couldn't possibly ever love Nicholas Aaronson. "Nick's an attorney. I was married to an attorney, but then I caught him in bed with Cynthia, and then I wasn't married anymore. And then there were the attorneys who handled our divorce. Despite the fact that Garth was the one who had cheated, they tried to blame all our problems on me. They tried to make me pay that slimeball alimony. They were brutal. I don't like brutal. I don't like attorneys, and I don't plan to marry again, either, especially not to another attorney."

"You like his eyes," Fern teased.

"Whose eyes?" Glory asked, feeling a headache hit her head with the force of a freight train plowing into a wall.

"Nick's eyes," Fern said.

"How do you—"

"We can read minds," Myrtle said. She shook her finger at Fern and Myrtle. "Though you both know Grace hates it when we let people know. She says it's rude."

"Pardon?" Glory asked weakly. She wasn't just losing control of the situation. She was also losing what little there was left of her mind.

"Oh, we don't read your deep, innermost thoughts, just those at the surface," Fern soothed. "And all three of us have heard your surface thoughts about Nick's eyes. You're right—they are so dark that it's hard to tell where the iris ends and the pupil begins."

"Nick, say something," Glory said. She wasn't losing her mind—she'd lost it. The process had started when she walked in on Garth and his bimbette. She'd quit her job—a job she loved—picked up and moved to a new city to start a new life. From corporate exec to waitress...yep, she was crazy all right.

"No you didn't," Fern said.

"Didn't what?" Glory felt lost.

"Love your job."

Glory squealed, "Nick!"

Shaking his head, as if awaking from a stupor, he said, "I don't know what the three of you are up to, but I don't care. You're not fairy godmothers. I'm not your fairy godchild and neither were my siblings."

"Actually, Max wasn't a godchild, Grace was." Myrtle just grinned up at him. "You can call them and ask them about us."

Nick totally ignored her and continued, "And I am not, and never will be, in love with Glory." With that, he stood up and stormed from the building.

The coward, Glory thought as she watched Nick flee. He'd just left her with three certifiably nuts, middle-aged ladies. That would teach her to trust an attorney. Even one with sexy eyes.

"What on earth are the three of you up to?" She scowled at her employees.

"Like we said, we're Nick's fairy godmothers. Fiona's too," Myrtle said. "Her case is especially difficult, and we're working on it as fast as we can, but obviously not fast enough for her."

"The reason you didn't fill out job applications is because you've all escaped from some nut-house, right?"

"Glory," Fern tsked. "Have we ever done anything that hurt you?"

"You mean other than the time Blossom's staple gun missed the upholstery and caught my finger?"

"Glory." Blossom's voice sounded watery, as if she were on the verge of tears. "You know that was an accident. Nick might be our godchild, and we do love him, but we love you, too."

"I just think—"

"Don't make any rash decisions," Myrtle ordered "You know when you worked for Michaelson's you always tried to sleep on major business matters before deciding. Well, we're part of your new business, and you shouldn't say or do something until you've had a chance to think about it."

"I don't need—"

"But you do. You need us helping in the restaurant, and you need Nick. You just don't know it yet."

"But—"

"Go home and go to sleep, Glory."

She didn't intend to obey—she was the boss after all. But she found herself home in bed before she knew what happened. If she didn't know better than to believe in fairies, she'd almost say they'd cast a spell on her.

No, she thought sluggishly as she drifted off to sleep. Fairies, magic and especially happily-ever-afters only existed in books.

***

Glory Chambers was taking charge of her life and her business. Her first charge was going to be against three supposed fairies. She was going to ship them all back to "Never-Never Land."

No, that was Peter Pan.

"Fairyland." That's where she'd ship them. She pulled

her car into the small reserved space behind the restaurant and sighed.

She'd spent her night imagining all the many ways she could fire the women. And all her fantasies ended with the three of them slinking out the door and never being seen again. Unfortunately, as tempting an idea as sending her three *fairy* employees packing was, Glory knew she wasn't going to do it. They had pitched in and helped get the restaurant cleaned up and opened.

Oh, they may have a mishap or two, but there was no way Glory could have done it all. The three women might be slightly off-center, but they were Glory's responsibility now. That sense of responsibility wouldn't allow her to send them back to wherever it was they came from.

So she wasn't going to fire them, but she was going to have a talk with them. Glory waited for an after breakfast lull before the lunch crowd started coming, but there wasn't one.

Lucky for them, Glory thought as she put on a fresh pot of coffee.

"Yeah, lucky for us," Myrtle whispered as she filled a mug to the brim with coffee.

Glory whirled around. "Lucky for you what?"

"Lucky that things have been so busy. Otherwise, we'd be getting your lecture." Myrtle paused a moment. "You thought about firing us, but if you fire us just for being fairies, you'd be discriminating. I mean, we've done our jobs and done them well. Just because we're fairies doesn't mean we don't do quality work."

At Glory's frown, Myrtle hastened to add, "Well, except for a small kitchen fire, a few broken dishes and a couple mixed up orders, our work has been above reproach."

"I don't think there are any laws on the books against discriminating against fairies." Glory grabbed the spray bottle of disinfectant and gave the counter a healthy squirt.

"You could call Nick and check." That Myrtle was hoping

she'd call Nick was obvious from her tone of voice.

"I'm not calling Nick. I know what you're up to, but I'm not falling for it. I'm not falling for Nick, and you can't make me."

"Oh, honey, you're right, we can't. We may have gotten the council to change a couple of the rules, but the rule about not being able to manipulate people's emotions is carved in stone. Anything you feel for Nick is totally your own. No magic involved. Love is magic enough on its own."

"I'm not in love with Nick. I will never be in love with Nick."

"If you say so."

"I say so." She might think Nick was good-looking—any woman would, what with his dark hair and even darker eyes—eyes so dark a woman could sink into their depths and never emerge. Eyes so dark she might see herself reflected in them if his face was over hers, peering into her soul. Eyes that—

Glory shut off the thoughts of Nick's dreamy eyes. She wasn't interested.

"Pardon me, miss," a customer at the counter called.

Glory turned her thoughts away from Nick Aaronson and back to work, aware that the interruption was giving Myrtle a chance to escape. Well, let her, because Glory would have her talk with all three of them after the store had closed. They could run, but they couldn't hide.

As she was giving the customer a quick coffee refill the postman walked into the restaurant."Excuse me, miss?"

"May I help you?" She turned and set the coffee pot back on the burner.

"I've got a certified letter for you." He reached in his bag and withdrew a large manilla envelope and clipboard.

"I'll sign for it." Glory reached for both.

He pulled the envelope back. "Are you Myrtle?"

"No, I'm Glory Chambers, the owner." The owner. The *boss*. Too bad she forgot that with Myrtle and her two cohorts.

"Sorry. This has to be signed for by a Myrtle."

"Myrtle who?" If the "fairies" wouldn't give her any information, she'd have to get it any way she could.

"No last name. Just Myrtle. Sort of like Cher, or Madonna, I guess. Is she some star?"

"Star isn't the word I'd use," Glory mumbled.

"Just what word would you use, Glory?" Myrtle asked from behind her.

Glory whirled around and came face-to-face with her redheaded employee. "Would you stop sneaking up behind me today!"

Myrtle didn't even bother to respond. Instead she turned to the postman and smiled. "I'm Myrtle."

"This is for you. You have to sign." He thrust a clipboard at her, and Myrtle scribbled her name.

Glory leaned over her shoulder to see what she signed. Her name...just her first name. "Have a good day," the postman said with a small wink.

"He was flirting with you," Glory said, as he walked out of the building.

"And why wouldn't he flirt with me? Why, in my younger days I had men lined up just waiting for a chance to take me on a date."

Myrtle tore open the envelope and without a word handed the contents to Glory.

"What is it?" Glory asked as she scanned the very legal looking document.

"It's official. We're being sued."

***

"He'll be with you shortly," Nick's receptionist promised.

Glory took a seat, wondering if she should wait or slink out of there while the slinking was good. "Have you worked for Nick long?" she asked in a bid to start a conversation that would make her forget how worried she was. That was the only reason she asked. It had nothing to do with a curiosity about Nick Aaronson.

The middled-aged brunette nodded. "I've been with him since he started. You couldn't have picked a better attorney."

Not waiting for Glory to respond, and obviously warming to a much-loved topic, she went on in a rush. "Did you know over twenty percent of his cases are pro-bono? He says he didn't go into law to get rich, but to make a difference."

The woman paused a moment, her face growing more serious as she said, "And sometimes that need to make a difference takes a toll. He's had a bad time of it lately. Too many clients he can't believe in, he says. I keep hoping someone special will come along and—"

The phone rang, stopping the chatty receptionist mid-sentence. Pro-bono work? She couldn't remember Garth ever volunteering to do anything, and doubted making a difference had anything to do with Garth getting into law.

A few muffled responses, and the receptionist looked at Glory and said, "You can go in now."

She might be making changes in her life, but she hoped there was still enough of the old-Glory's persuasiveness left in her to convince Nick he had to take this case.

Deciding to start the meeting on the offensive, she entered and said, "Nick, I'm not going to beat around the bush. You know why I'm here. You have to help them." She didn't need to explain who *them* referred to. They both knew.

Nick's offices weren't exactly what Glory would have imagined. She would have guessed that simple, elegant and functional office would have suited Nick. Instead, his office was in one of Erie's older historical homes. There was a richness and a plushness that didn't quite seem to fit with what she knew of Nick. Just as donating so much of time to pro-bono work didn't quite jive with what she thought she knew about this man—not that she knew a lot about Nick.

Not that she wanted to know more, despite what the fairies wanted.

Despite the fact she didn't believe for one minute her employees were fairy godmothers, she realized she'd started thinking for them as fairies. Glory gave herself a mental shake. That would have to stop.

Nick sat across the desk, looking especially ferocious but saying nothing. If they were indeed trapped in a fairy tale, Glory would say that at that moment he looked more like the Big Bad Wolf than Prince Charming.

"They need you," she pressed. "You have to help them."

"I don't have to do anything. And I don't want to be the attorney for three fairies."

Why was he being so stubborn? Glory answered her unspoken question herself—because he was a man. Darn the entire race.

When Myrtle had handed her the letter, Glory knew she was going to help them. They might have fairy-delusions, but they had good hearts. And when she'd needed them, they'd been there. How could she not be there now when they needed her?

And helping them meant getting them an attorney—getting them Nick Aaronson. He was the only attorney she knew, and the saying went *the devil you know beats the devil you don't.*

"I don't know who else to turn to." It galled her to admit that.

"Don't *turn.* Just dump the lot and hire someone else to work at the restaurant. People with real last names, social security numbers and addresses." He tossed the letter back across his desk at her. "Don't hire any more fairies, and don't expect me to help with the three you already have."

"Nick!" The fact that Myrtle, Fern and Blossom thought she and Nick were meant to be together just proved they weren't fairy godmothers. There was no way Glory was going to fall for such a frustratingly obnoxious man. Where was the man *who wants to make a difference* his receptionist was telling her about?

"Glory, don't you see, this is just a ploy to get the two of us together."

"How will defending Myrtle, Fern and Blossom get us together?" She pushed the letter back at him.

"I'll have to see them, and that means I'll have to see you. That's their plan. They're going to keep forcing us together until we finally give in and fall in love." He pushed the letter back at her with such force that it almost skittered off the desk. "And I don't plan on falling in love."

Glory stopped the letter with the palm of her hand and batted it back to him. "Nick, you're talking as if you believe they're really fairies. You don't, do you? I mean, it's just some delusion all three of them share."

Nick paused, his hand on the letter. No, he didn't believe in fairies, but it seemed as if his siblings and their spouses did. Joy and Max both swore that Myrtle, Fern and Blossom were the real deal—one hundred percent, bonafide fairy godmothers.

"No," he said slowly. "I don't believe in fairies, miracles, happily-ever-afters, or matches made in heaven. Or in Fairyland for that matter. Life is what we make of it. Magic and miracles, those are just things people who haven't made anything of their lives believe in." He pushed the letter back across the desk. "I've made my life into exactly what I want it to be. I don't need any crutches. And I especially don't need any fairies."

"Right. Magic and miracles are just tools for the weak-minded and the weak-willed. That being said, I still need an attorney." Glory shuttled the piece of paper, which was looking decidedly worse for wear, back at Nick.

"You don't need an attorney. They need an attorney." That was the truth. Glory didn't have to be here. And yet here she was, arguing on behalf of three crazy women. A spark of admiration lit in Nick. But he wasn't about to let her sway him to her cause.

"They, Glory—not you—need an attorney. Better yet, all four of you need a psychiatrist. I'd send you to Max, but I'm worried about his sanity these days." A psychiatrist who believed in fairy godmothers? What would the AMA make of that?

"Glory, this," he waved the ragged piece of paper, "isn't about you."

"Wrong. For better or worse, those three signed on with the restaurant. They worked as hard as I did getting it opened. Now, for better or worse—and it looks like worse—they're my responsibility. So I need an attorney for them. I need you, Nick."

Though he knew she was just talking about legal expertise, the words hung heavily between them. *She needed him.* He liked the sound of that.

Oh, he wasn't about to fall in love with her, but Glory Chambers was glorious in her defense of fairies. She'd risen from her chair and was glaring down at him. She faced him across the desk, not the least bit intimidated by him, or even a little bit impressed. She wasn't here because she wanted to be here but because she needed him to represent the fairies.

He wouldn't mind hearing *I need you, Nick,* under other circumstances. But with all this talk about happily-ever-afters, he wasn't about to risk finding out just how glorious Glory Chambers could be. One night of passion would have Glory, the three pseudo-fairies and his entire family hearing wedding bells. No, a night of wild sex with Glory was out of the question, and because it was, staying as far away from her as he could get was a good course of action.

Last night he hadn't dreamed of Lola, and he hadn't dreamed of fairies. He'd dreamed of Glory—a wild and exhilarating dream that had haunted him all day. Now seeing her in his office passionately defending the fairies made him think his dreams were nowhere near as glorious as a real night with her would be.

"Glory, I can't represent fairies... or rather women who think they're fairies. Can you imagine what it would do to my reputation?"

"And do you imagine any other attorney in town who will defend them? Face it Aaronson, you're it."

"Then they're out of luck. I don't owe them anything." Realizing he was still fingering the letter, he thrust it back across the desk.

Glory caught it and held onto it this time. "You'd let three women get taken to the cleaners by some woman who bought into their delusion, just because you don't want to tarnish your reputation?"

"Yes."

"Nick." Behind that one word, just his name whispered softly and sadly, he heard her disappointment. And though it didn't make sense, disappointing Glory cut at him. She rose, letter clutched in her hand, and walked toward his office door.

"I'm sorry." Nick wasn't sure if he was sorry he'd disappointed her, or sorry he felt he had to disappoint her. But either way, he was sorry.

She turned, one hand holding the letter, the other on the doorknob. "Never mind. We'll do it without you."

"Do what?" He realized he'd risen from his chair and trailed her across the room. He didn't remember following her, but he must have because he was standing close enough to catch the scent of her perfume. Soft and floral. The scent didn't quite fit the tough image she tried to project.

An image of making love to glorious Glory in a flower-scented field flitted across his mind's eye. Glory, lying beneath him, her titian hair spread across the flowers, red against red. She was smiling at him. Not just one of those little social smiles she'd perfected, but a true, from-the-depths-of-her-soul sort of smile. He wanted to know what that kind of uninhibited smile would be like coming from Glory. He wanted to learn her body inside and out. But more dangerous than that, he wanted to know *her* inside and out.

He shut the thought off as quickly and firmly as he could. "What are you going to do?" he asked.

"I'll ask around town, and I'll find someone to represent them. Firing them and distancing myself from them might be the smart business move, but I can't do it. They might be slightly delusional, but they're basically sweet and hardworking women. I won't let them get taken to the cleaners. They pitched in and helped me get the restaurant open. They stood by me, and now I'll stand by them, even if I have to represent them myself."

"You're not an attorney." But he was. And as such he knew better than to study the determination that caused her lips to pucker ever so slightly. Her puckered lips made him think about kissing.

Kissing Glory. Making love to Glory. No! Both ideas were totally out of the question.

"I might not be an attorney, but I was married to one. I did pick up some useful information from Garth."

She still stood with one hand on the doorknob, as if ready to bolt if need be. Nick reached out and touched her elbow. "I know Bill Richards, the attorney representing this woman according to the letter of intent. He'll eat you alive."

"Do you have another suggestion?"

It wasn't Bill Richards eating her alive she had to worry about, Nick realized.

"One." Rather than pulling her into his arms, he simply leaned forward—his hand still on her elbow, the other hanging loosely at his side—and let his lips lightly brush hers. He paused and looked into her eyes, those startling blue eyes, waiting for some sign he should stop. When no sign came, he kissed her again, deeper and longer this time, still just touching her lips, leaving her a way out if she chose to take it.

She tasted of peppermint, some dim recess of his mind

registered. Peppermint and wild flowers. Red hair on red flowers. His dream came rushing back, only he was dreaming it awake—dreaming it with Glory.

He deepened the kiss, needing to get closer to her, as close as he could. He—

She ripped her elbow out of his grasp and drew back panting. "What do you think you're doing?"

"Kissing you?"

"Why?"

He shrugged. "I don't know." He didn't have a clue. Kissing Glory was the last thing he should be doing. His life didn't need complications, and Glory and her three fairies were COMPLICATIONS in all capital letters.

"Well, don't do it again."

"Was kissing me so bad?"

Glory looked as if she was going to tell him just how bad it was, but then she closed her mouth. He watched her mentally pull herself back together. "Just don't do it again." She turned and started to open the door.

Nick slammed his hand against it, shutting it. He should let her walk out of his life. Then he could forget his three *fairy godmothers,* forget the redhead who had taken over his every waking and dreaming thought, and just get on with life. But he knew he wasn't going to do that.

Damn.

"I'll do it."

She stopped and turned to face him, looking confused. "Do what? Represent the fairies?"

Nick wanted to say no, wanted to shout *hell no,* but instead he nodded. He wanted to know if Glory's look of confusion had to do with his offer to represent the fairies, or if she was confused by his kiss.

He wanted her to be confused by that kiss because it was sure as hell confusing him.

"Are you representing them because we kissed?"

"No. I have no idea why I kissed you like that, but I won't be doing it again. I'll represent them because you're right. No one else will."

"I know that they'll be thrilled." Her tone said that she was anything but.

"Let me finish. I'll do it if they swear they won't constantly try to throw us together. You and I have to have an understanding right up front that we might have kissed—"

"You kissed me. I didn't do anything."

Nick was gentleman enough not to mention she'd kissed him back—gentleman enough not to confess how much he had liked it. "I might have kissed you, but that doesn't mean I want to marry you. I'm not looking for happily-ever-afters. I'm not even looking for a happy-for-a-few-months. My life is full, and if I'm taking on this case it's just gotten even fuller. Nothing—absolutely nothing—ever-after-ish will develop between us."

Glory raised her hand and crossed her heart. "I have no interest in developing anything lasting with you. That much I can promise you."

"That's good enough for me. We're both clear on what we want, and more importantly, what we don't want. Set up an appointment with my secretary for tomorrow. We'll get started."

"Thanks, Nick. You won't regret this." She raced out of his office and shut the door as if she was afraid he'd change his mind.

"I already regret it," Nick whispered as his finger traced his lips, the same lips that had just kissed Glory Chambers. What had be been thinking?

***

"What were you thinking?" Glory whispered as she gazed at her reflection in the medicine cabinet mirror. She wasn't sure why she whispered. She was alone in the kitchen. Myrtle, Fern and Blossom were all in the dining room, leaving her a few peaceful minutes to collect herself before facing them.

She stared at her reflection. She looked the same as she had countless other mornings. She didn't look crazy. But she must be, because only a crazy person would let herself be kissed by Nicholas Aaronson. He was far too good-looking, far too sure of himself, and far too much an attorney. Add to that the fact they had fairy godmothers trying to set them up...well, there was no way her lips should be on his.

Lightly she trailed her finger across those lips that had so recently been attached to Nick Aaronson's.

No. She should keep her distance from Nick. And yet, she'd let him kiss her. Worse, she'd lied when she said he'd done all the kissing. The truth was she'd kissed him back. And a bigger truth was, it would have been very, very easy to continue kissing him.

"And I could have gone on kissing him for a long time," she whispered again.

Hiring fairy godmothers, talking to her reflection and kissing attorneys. Glory shook her head in disgust. She had definitely lost her mind and should be locked up with her employees.

She'd sworn to Nick that she had no interest in him outside of his ability to defend the fairies. Though she had always thought of herself as honest to a fault, it was a lie.

A humdinger of a lie.

She could be interested in Nick if she gave herself half a chance. He might be an attorney, but there was something different about him, something Garth and their divorce attorneys had lacked.

Yes, it was possible that she could overlook Nick's attorney-ness, but she wasn't going to give herself a chance. He'd made it clear he wasn't interested in her, and she had already decided she was taking some time off from men. Her life had enough complications—she'd just walked away from a career and a marriage, and she was in the middle of re-creating herself.

If that wasn't enough, she'd hired three fairy godmothers who liked to blow things up. No, she didn't need a man muddling the mix, especially not a man like Nick.

He probably had a hundred women who were little more than notches on his briefcase. He wouldn't be seriously interested in a frizzy, red-haired restauranteur. She plucked at one of her runaway curls. No, Nick wouldn't be interested at all, which was just fine with her since she wasn't interested in him either.

"Sure you are," Myrtle said.

Glory turned and realized she wasn't alone any longer. Her three employees stood in a row watching her, expectation written on all three faces.

"Sure I am what?" she hedged.

"Interested in Nick," Blossom said, a hand clutched to her chest. "It's so romantic."

"And don't you worry, honey. He's interested, too. It's just he's as stubborn as you and doesn't want to admit it," Fern added.

"I'm not stubborn."

"Oh? That's not what the people at Michaelson's said," Myrtle said.

"I was vice-president. I was assertive and decisive and focused—not stubborn."

"And that's not what your husband said." Fern grimaced as she mentioned Garth.

Glory's expression echoed Ferns. "Garth was a lying rat, so you can't believe anything he said."

"Neither can you," Myrtle said softly.

"Neither can I what?" Talking to the three of them was like talking in a giant circle. They made Glory's head spin.

"You can't believe anything Garth said," Myrtle assured her.

"You're not a bossy, demanding woman who doesn't

know how to please a man," Blossom said breathlessly. "Why, just that one little kiss pleased Nick a lot, and—"

"How did you know about the kiss?" Glory asked sharply.

"Why, it's written all over your face," Myrtle assured her. "Knowing you kissed Nick doesn't take a fairy godmother's ability to read thoughts."

"Yeah, it's sort of blinking like a neon sign." Blossom's hands framed her face. "I kissed Nick...I kissed Nick...I kissed Nick."

Fern chuckled. "And right after that, it blinks...and I liked it...and I liked it...and I—"

"Cut that out. I don't know how you know we kissed, but it's none of your business. And for the record, he kissed me. I didn't kiss him back, and I most certainly didn't like it."

"Glory, people might say you're stubborn, and you are, but they've never said you're a liar. So why are you starting now?" Myrtle asked.

"You can't lie to us anyway," Fern assured her.

"And you shouldn't lie to yourself," Blossom added. "You liked kissing Nick."

"And, if it will make you feel better, he liked kissing you, too," Myrtle said.

"Oh, he didn't like *liking it* any more than you do, but he did—like it, I mean," Fern added.

"Could the three of you stop talking in circles? You're making my head hurt. And whether or not either of us liked it doesn't matter. What matters is there will be no more kissing between Nick and me."

"Tsk, tsk, tsk," Fern clicked. "There you go again, telling lies."

"There won't be any more kissing," Glory promised herself more than the fairies.

Blossom looked worried. "There has to be."

"Why?"

"Because you and Nick are meant for each other. That's

why you can't stay away from each other," Fern said.

"We can't stay away from each other because three interfering women who think they're fairies got themselves sued. By the way, Nick agreed to represent you."

"We know." One blonde, one brunette and one red head bobbed up and down in unison.

"How do you—never mind, I don't want to know. You've got a meeting with him tomorrow."

"We have a meeting." Myrtle gestured to all four of them.

"No way. I got you an attorney, and now I'm done. Someone will have to stay and hold down the fort here. I can't afford to close the restaurant down after it just opened."

"Glory, we need you," Blossom said.

"We thought you were our friend." There was admonishment in Fern's voice.

"Even though you were thinking about firing us, we knew you never would. You might think we're nuts, but you like us," Myrtle said, sure in that assessment.

Damned if they weren't right, but Glory wasn't about to admit it. "I can't close down the restaurant."

"You don't have to," Myrtle promised.

"Then how—"

Fern cut off Glory's argument. "We arranged for help."

"What kind of help?" Glory couldn't help thinking of all the "help" her three employees had given the restaurant...help that had required a lot of Band-Aids, plaster and even a fire extinguisher. She wasn't sure if the restaurant could survive more *help.*

Glory wasn't sure she could, either.

"Oh, the best kind of help. Friends are riding to the rescue even as we speak." Blossom looked rather swoony again. Swooning seemed to be a specialty of the small blonde's.

"What friends?"

Myrtle patted Glory's back. "Don't worry. The restaurant will be in good hands."

***

The next morning at precisely nine-thirty, the fairies' *friends* arrived.

"Aren't you—"

"Nick's sister, Joy," said the small brunette. "Nice to meet you. This is my husband, Gabriel." The tall man with auburn hair and a sweet smile nodded.

"And I'm Nick's sister-in-law, Grace," said the blonde. "And this is his brother, Max." Glory could see the resemblance between Max and Nick. Both had dark complexions and dark hair. They also had similar builds. Max was a good-looking enough man, but he didn't hold a candle to Nick.

Not that Glory was holding a candle for Nick, or holding anything else for him, either. She eyed the four. "Why are you here?"

"We're going to run things while you all meet with Nick, and we'll fill in for the trial, too," said Grace.

"But—"

"No, buts, Glory. We might not be experts, but we'll handle things. And we'll probably do it with less property or bodily damage than your current employees," Max said with a grin.

"What do you know about restaurants?"

"Let's see, you've got a CEO, the head of a charitable organization, a psychiatrist, and a writer. There's not much we can't handle," said Joy. "And lucky for you, I can cook. We'll all juggle our schedules and see to it there's always a couple of us here."

"Besides," said Myrtle coming into the dining room through the kitchen door, "they know as much about running a restaurant as the vice-president of an international corporation."

"Myrtle?" the two men gasped in unison.

Max rushed forward and hugged the small redhead.

"Finally, I get to see you. You don't know how many times I tried to imagine how you look."

"And what do you think?" the redhead asked with laughter in her voice.

"You look better than I imagined." He hugged her again, then held her at arm's length and said, "We need you to explain this change in the rules."

"Let her explain later," said Gabriel, pushing Max out of the way. He hugged Myrtle as well. "I know I didn't hear about your help until after the fact, but I owe the three of you a huge thanks."

Myrtle chuckled. "You're welcome, Gabriel. And Max, changing the rules was tough. We'll tell you the whole story later, I swear. But right now we have an appointment."

Fern and Blossom rushed from the kitchen and into Max's and Gabriel's arms. The two couples and the three fairies babbled away. Glory had a hard time keeping up with what was being said. Not that she cared. She'd done her duty. She'd found the fairies legal representation. She didn't need to go to this meeting.

And listening to the two couples go on and on about the way the fairies had helped them find love, Glory was certain she didn't want to see Nick any time soon. She'd admitted to herself that she might be attracted to him. And yesterday, seeing how he took on a case he didn't want—a case that might make him a laughing stock in the legal community—she'd found that he was a man whose principles she admired as well. But even if she lusted after him and was discovering he was an attorney with a conscience, she didn't love him and she didn't want to love him.

"Max, Grace, Gabriel and Joy, I want to thank you all for coming," she said. "But, I'm not the one being sued. And I don't need to be at this meeting."

"Listen, we all did our time with the girls. It's your turn," said Grace. Before Glory could ask what she meant, she went on, "They need you. Are you going to just walk away from that?"

"Why are you doing this?" Glory asked, confused. "You've all got careers, things you should be seeing to. Running a small diner doesn't make sense. I don't understand."

Joy reached out and squeezed Glory's hand. "You're almost family, and this is what family does...they step in and help when it's needed. Even if it's not especially wanted."

"We're staying," both men said together.

Glory knew when to admit defeat. Three fairies and four of Nick's relatives were more than any one person could face. "Fine. I'm going."

"Good," came seven voices.

Glory gathered her things and loaded the three fairies into her car. How on earth had she gotten herself into this situation? Last year her life had been perfectly normal. She'd been married and working at a job she understood, even if she didn't always like it. Now she was running a restaurant, working with fairy godmothers and kissing attorneys.

Glory had no idea how she had ended up here. She was surrounded by crazy old ladies who had even crazier friends. If she wasn't careful, Glory would end up joining the sanity-challenged ranks.

Five

Nick stared at the four women and wondered for the hundredth time how he had gotten himself into this position.

He was crazy. That was the only explanation.

But crazy or not, he was a professional. And professional was exactly how he planned to run this meeting and the entire case.

"Ladies, please have a seat. We have an informal meeting with Ms. Fayette and her attorney later this week. Bill and I both agree that avoiding the courtroom is to both our clients' benefit, so we're hoping to hammer things out ourselves and avoid the publicity."

Myrtle looked nervous. "But, Nick—"

"Stop," he said sharply, sensing an argument brewing.

The three fairies' faces fell at his harsh tone. Nick felt a spurt of guilt, but he didn't feel guilty enough to be more gentle. "I think we had better start by laying down some rules. I didn't want this case, but I took it. Now I'm running things. That's the first thing all of you have to remember. Don't talk unless you're spoken to, don't offer any information, and don't try to throw Glory and me together. We are both adults, and we don't need your help getting together if we want to, which we don't."

"Oh, you want to. That kiss proved that. And yes, you do need our help," Blossom said. "We've had some tough cases in the past, but you two take the cake. You're both stubborn, bossy and convinced you'll never find true love. You're real tough."

"Well, not as hard as Fiona," Fern pointed out.

"You can say that again," Blossom said. "You'd think she'd appreciate all we've done for her. But does she?"

"No, and you know Ber—"

"Fern!" Myrtle squawked. "You almost gave it away. You know better than that. I expect more from you. Blossom's the one who usually can't keep her mouth shut."

"Hey!" Blossom yelled. "I resent that."

"No, dear, you resemble that," Myrtle grumbled.

"Sorry, Myrtle," Fern mumbled, obviously contrite.

Nick sat next to Glory, both of them listening to the fairies' circular conversation.

"Ladies," he warned. Most people would have heard it and been worried, but these three just laughed at him.

"You can't intimidate us with that tone, young man." Myrtle waggled a finger in his direction.

"It would take something more than that to scare us," Blossom said. "Like the first time we met Rocky. We didn't know what to make of her when June got dumped in the same cell with her. I'll admit, I was more than just a little afraid then." Blossom paused then added, "And I'll confess I was afraid of what June was going to do to us when she got out."

"I wasn't afraid of June or Rocky," Fern said. "It would take Ber—"

"Fern!" Myrtle shouted.

"Sorry." The brunette looked woebegone. "I don't know what's come over me. I guess it's this entire trial business. I'm not used to being sued."

"Now, about the case. We're going to settle this thing as quickly as possible." Nick was going to get control of this situation, even if it killed him. He was an attorney. He should be capable of controlling three old ladies.

Myrtle frowned. "We're not old."

"And we don't want to settle out of court," Fern added.

"What do you mean you don't want to settle out of court?" Nick asked, desperately trying to keep up with the twists and turns that conversing with his three clients seemed to take.

"Nick, are you having problems with your hearing?" Blossom looked concerned. "We said, we want a trial."

"We don't just *want* a trial," Myrtle corrected her. "We *have to have* a trial."

"Myrtle, that's ridiculous." Nick knew taking this particular case to trial wasn't just ill-advised, it was suicide. Myrtle, Fern and Blossom wouldn't just lose the case, they'd probably find themselves committed. "If you take this to trial, you're exposing yourself to the press."

"We need to take this to court," Myrtle stubbornly maintained.

"But if we don't settle out of court, you could lose everything," he argued.

"Honey, we don't have anything." Fern laughed. "Fairies aren't materialistic. We know that there are more important things in life than *things.* Losing everything when you own nothing isn't much of a risk."

"And we'll lose a lot more if we don't take this to court," Blossom added.

Nick was their attorney and, by God, they were going to listen to his advice. "But—"

"We want a judge to decide our case." Myrtle waited for his next volley.

"No you don't." Nick folded his arms. They wanted to draw the battle lines, well so be it. If he was stuck representing them, he wasn't about to lose the case. He hated losing. "No. You absolutely do not want to take this in front of a judge."

"Yes we do," the three said in unison. All three fairy faces were stubbornly set.

Blossom's was the first to soften. "He's worried about

us," she whispered to Glory.

"Of course he is," Glory said. "He's your attorney. We're paying him to be worried about you."

Nick shot her an appreciative look. He had a feeling he was going to need her as an ally if he was going to win this case.

He echoed Glory's assurances. "Of course I'm worried.. You're clients. That's my job, to worry and look out for you."

"That's sweet." Blossom elbowed Glory. "Isn't that sweet, Glory?"

"Nick's not being sweet. He's just doing what he's paid to do." There was no softness in Glory's expression when she looked at him. "And if Nick says your best interests will be served by dealing with Fiona out of court, then I'd listen."

"We can't do that. Honestly." Fern crossed her heart. "We know you both think we're being difficult, and we can't explain why, but this case has to be heard by a judge."

"And I can't talk you into just listening to what Fiona wants?" Nick asked wearily.

Weary? Hell, he was exhausted by just a short meeting with the four women. How was he going to feel by the end of the case?

"I'm sorry, Nick. We're all sorry."

Myrtle actually looked as if she was sincere, but Nick suspected they were just making things difficult because...well, hell if he knew why they were being difficult, but he was sure they had a reason. He had a feeling that despite their air-head facade Myrtle, Fern and Blossom generally had reasons for everything they did.

Myrtle said, "But our being sorry doesn't change things. We need to have a judge hear the case."

Nick sensed his utter defeat on the issue of settling out of court. "So what about a defense?"

"There are people who will stand up for us," Myrtle assured him. "They'll testify on our behalf."

"Who?"

"You sister and brother, and their spouses, for example." Fern promised.

"You've got to be kidding." Oh, he could see the headlines now. *Prominent Erie family seeing fairies—film at eleven.*

"We told you that we had a hand in their getting together." Myrtle had the same obstinate look in her eye that his mother frequently got when she was determined to have her own way. "Didn't you ask them?"

"What would I say? *Pardon me, Max and Joy, but did three fairy godmothers set you and your spouses up?"* Nick wasn't going to admit, especially in front of Glory, that he didn't have to ask his brother and sister since they'd both told him their fairy tales. He wasn't sure why they were playing into Myrtle, Fern and Blossom's delusions, but he didn't believe any of them.

"Listening to their stories is a start." Fern patted his hand. "They're good friends, and they'll testify on our behalf."

"And having a psychiatrist say you're not delusional, but are real fairies should help," Blossom said, suddenly chipper.

"But even if the court will allow that you are fairies—and I find that highly doubtful—what about Fiona? Does she have a case?"

"We did promise her a happily-ever-after," Myrtle allowed. "And the truth of the matter is she hasn't gotten one yet. I imagine the wait could cause some emotional distress."

"Though if she was honest," Blossom added, "Fiona would have to admit she's spent most her life distressed. It comes from not fitting in."

"And it's hard to fit into a world you were never meant to be in," Fern said sagely.

"So, even though she might have experienced emotional distress before we came along, I imagine it's been worse since we introduced ourselves," Myrtle finished.

Nick slammed his pen down on his pad of paper. "So

you're admitting her claims have merit?"

"Oh, no, we're not admitting that," Fern argued. "You see, we did promise her a happily-ever-after, but we never said we'd given up. As a matter of fact—"

"Fern!" Blossom and Myrtle yelled in unison.

The brunette clapped a hand over her mouth and sank back in her chair.

"Let's just say that we're not done with Fiona Fayette." Myrtle's cryptic statement had all three women grinning and nodding their heads in unison.

"Not by a long shot," Fern added.

"Listen, the three of you are to stay away from her." Nick picked up his pen and again slammed it onto the pad of paper for emphasis. "No trying to set her up. No midnight visits in her dreams. No—"

"You believe us?" Blossom sounded excited.

"Pardon?" Nick asked.

"You just admitted you'd seen us in your dreams," Myrtle caught the verbal slip, and with the instincts of an attorney, hammered out a rapid question. "How else would you explain our being in your dreams if we aren't fairies?"

"I'm nuts. That's how I'd explain it. But, since I'm not the one on trial, I don't have to explain anything."

Blossom reached out and patted his hand. "But—"

"Listen, if we're taking this to trial, I have to figure out some defense before the ball's rolling."

"I think you'll find it will roll pretty fast." Myrtle looked like a cat who had secretly eaten the canary.

"Ha." Nick realized that was a less-than-adult response and hastily added, "That shows what you know about the court system. This could take years."

"But it won't." Fern sounded sure of herself.

"We can't afford to wait that long." Blossom nervously nibbled a fingernail. "This has waited long enough."

Glory had watched with delight as Nick battled the fairies.

Served him right. How dare he kiss her?

She wanted revenge, and letting the three women go to town on him—letting them twist everything he said until he didn't know if he was coming or going—seemed a good way to accomplish it. Since kissing him, she'd felt twisted around and unsure of whether she was coming or going.

Going. That's exactly what she should be doing. Going to the nearest exit and getting away from the infuriating man and the three wanna-be-fairy-godmothers.

Instead, she was sitting in an attorney's office, watching the entertaining battle, letting virtual strangers run her restaurant...and fantasizing about kissing Nick again. She wasn't sure quite how it had happened, but as she watched him try to get a straight answer out of the fairies she couldn't help noticing how very kissable his lips were.

Strong. Those lips, pursed with annoyance, inspired trust. But Glory sadly admitted to herself that she wasn't ready to trust anyone—especially not another attorney. Besides, Nick was too opinionated. Too sure of himself. Too...damn sexy for his own good.

Too damn sexy for her own good.

And yet, though he was opinionated and too sexy for his own good, Nick Aaronson wasn't what she had expected. He cared about Myrtle, Fern and Blossom. He might think they were crazy as proverbial bed-bugs, but he was putting his career on the line to defend them anyway. She couldn't imagine Garth ever taking that type of risk for anyone. She couldn't imagine the attorneys who had handled her divorce defending fairies, either.

But Nick Aaronson was doing just that.

He had a kind heart, which in Glory's opinion was even sexier than his very kissable lips, which was saying something because those lips were very sexy and tempting. She could almost feel them—

"Glory?"

She realized she was being spoken to and pulled her gaze away from Nick's lips. "Pardon?"

"Are you going to sit there staring at me, or you going to help?" Nick demanded.

"Help with what?"

"Controlling your employees."

"When they're in the restaurant, they're my worry. When they're here, they're all yours. I just showed up for moral support." And how on earth did Nick expect her to control three fairies when she couldn't control her own thoughts? The last thing she should be thinking about was kissing Nick, but there it was—she was not only thinking about kissing him, she was fantasizing about it.

"Well, let me just say you're not being very supportive."

"Their moral support, not yours. I'm sure you're used to handling things on your own, so I doubt you need my help." But she'd love to help—help herself to another taste of Nick Aaronson's lips.

"But you claimed you needed my help when you asked me to take this case."

"No. I said *they* needed your help. I don't need anyone."

"Glory Chambers doesn't need anyone?" he repeated doubtfully.

"Once upon a time I might have thought I did, but not anymore." She didn't need anyone, not even a gorgeous man with a big heart. And she especially didn't need Nick's kisses.

Myrtle cleared her throat. "Are we done for now? We should get back to the restaurant—"

"I hate it when you two fight," Blossom interrupted, frowning at Nick and Glory.

"We weren't fighting," Glory assured her.

"Sure you were. Both of you seem to think standing alone makes you stronger, but actually letting someone else stand with you can only make you stronger."

"No trying to fix us up," Nick reminded Blossom. "I'm

not interested, and neither is Glory. Right, Glory?"

"Right. I'm not interested at all." Glory should have felt relieved to hear Nick echo her feelings so succinctly. She wasn't interested. He might be different from other attorneys, and he might have lusciously kissable lips, but she wasn't interested in a repeat performance. At least not very interested.

She had to get away from Nick and whatever spell he was casting over her. She stood. "And Myrtle's right. We should get back to the restaurant, so if you're done..."

"I'm done for today. But we still have questions that need answered. I feel like all I got today was a runaround."

"Why, Nick, we answered everything you asked," Myrtle said indignantly.

"Maybe you should find better questions next time," Blossom offered.

"Maybe I should find better clients next time," Nick muttered as the four women marched out of his office.

He didn't have anything going on at the courthouse, so he spent the day working in his office. But he couldn't take his eye off the folder he'd come to think of as the *fairy file.* Being sued for not producing a happily-ever-after. He was pretty sure that no matter how he searched he wouldn't find any precedence in this case. The only way to win was not to fight, despite what the fairies said. He decided to call Bill.

"Looks like we'll be facing off again," he said without preamble. "I'm having trouble talking them into settling."

"How on earth did they rope you into representing them?" That Bill found the situation humorous was evident in his tone.

"I was going to ask you the same thing about this Fayette woman. I mean, come on Bill, she's suing for a happily-ever-after?"

"I've known the girl since she was a babe. Her father was my partner. Such a pretty little thing. Her parents had tried forever to have a child, but they couldn't. The day they brought that baby home was the happiest day of their lives. And they loved her, and she loved them . . ."

Nick could hear Bill's hesitation as the sentence trailed off.

"But?" he prompted.

"But she always marched to the beat of a different drum. She couldn't fit into their family, or anywhere else for that matter. I think that's why your clients hurt her so badly. She wanted to believe in them, wanted to believe that finally she was going to find someone she fit with." He paused, then added, "I'm no psychiatrist, but that's the way I see it."

"Bill, these three women are different, but they're not malicious. I don't think they meant to hurt her."

"Maybe not, but she has a right to be compensated. They made promises that they had no way of delivering."

"Well, they're adamant about not settling. They want a trial."

"You're their attorney. You can't convince them that it's in their best interest to see this put to rest as quietly as possible?"

"You know it's best for your client as well," Nick felt obliged to point out.

"Maybe," Bill muttered.

"Definitely. Believing in fairy godmothers can't be very sane." Which is why Nick had no intentions of believing the three ladies' claims. But he was their attorney, and if they told him they were fairy godmothers, then he'd play along and support their right to be fairies, all the way to the Supreme Court. He even referred to them as the fairies. But representing and referring didn't have anything to do with believing.

He didn't—he *wouldn't*—believe.

"Looks like I'll be seeing you in court then, counselor."

Nick massaged his pounding temple. This case could get ugly. "Sorry about that, Bill."

"Me to."

***

"What do you mean, we've got a date?" Getting a court date should have taken months.

The Court Administrator's assistant, Clancy Thomas, shrugged. "Just what I said. Two weeks from tomorrow. The Honorable Judge Bernard Fallon will be presiding."

"Who?"

"Annette Anderson is pregnant—"

"Since when?" Nick had dealt with Judge Anderson often in the past and thought he was pretty much abreast of courthouse gossip, but he'd heard nothing about her pregnancy.

"Since about three months ago. The doctor said it's triplets, and she's on complete bed rest. So, the AOPC—Administrative Office of Pennsylvania Courts—assigned us Judge Fallon for the duration. He's from some little town down near Philly."

"But that doesn't explain how fast—"

"Two weeks, Nick."

Two weeks to find some defense for fairies who hadn't provided a happily-ever-after? "But I haven't had time—"

"You'll have to find time because you've got two weeks." Clancy offered him a sympathetic smile.

Sympathy wasn't what Nick needed. More time, that's what he needed. That, or non-fairy clients. Either would do.

"What do you know about the judge?" he asked, resigned to his fate.

"Only what the AOPC sent. He's retired and no one knows much about him, but he's qualified on paper."

"Come on, you've got to know something more than that." Sometimes it felt more like he worked on a soap opera than in the court system. Everyone knew everything about everyone, and most didn't hesitate to share the information.

"He's a ghost, Nick. No one knows anything about him, other than the AOPC is sending him to us, and he's hearing your case."

“Thanks anyway, Clancy.”

As Nick left the courthouse, his couldn’t keep from glancing across the street to Glory’s Chambers. How on earth had he gotten himself into this mess?

Six

"Baked beans do not make a nutritionally balanced meal, Mr. Foster."

"Now, Glory. Nag, nag, nag. That's all you seem to do. Why can't you be sweet and compliant like your aunt was?" The elderly gentleman nervously wiped a hand over his furrowed brow.

Glory had grown fond of the old man. He'd been a regular since the first day Glory's Chambers had opened. He'd told her stories of the aunt she'd never known who had run The Coffee House for years. Glory was sorry she hadn't known her aunt, and she appreciated Mr. Foster's patronage and friendship. But not enough to bring him baked beans for lunch. They had this argument nearly every day, and every time she won.

Mr. Foster enjoyed the confrontations, and since the customer was always right, she was happy to play along.

"Ah, now, Mr. Foster, people have been asking why I wasn't sweet since I was a girl. Fact is, I don't know what the answer is, but I do know you won't be eating just baked beans today. They're not even on the menu."

"Your aunt used to buy cans of them for me."

"Well, since I'm not my aunt, we're going to have to make a deal. I'll bring you a nice big salad and a glass of milk. And, if you behave and eat your lunch, I'll see if Fern will slice you an extra thick piece of chocolate cake. It's your favorite, right?" Glory could see the battle was over.

"I guess a salad might taste good," the old man allowed.

"You just hang tight, and I'll see to it that it does." Glory turned around and walked into the kitchen. She took one of Fern's salads and started piling extra raw vegetables on top of it. She was going to pack as much nutrition as possible into the salad.

The bowl was just too small, she decided as things began overflowing. She dug through the cabinet until she found a bigger one.

"Just what do you think you're doing?" Fern asked.

"I'm making a salad for Mr. Foster." The man looked as if he needed all the nutrition she could pack into each meal.

"Who?" Fern asked innocently, much too innocently.

"You know, older gentleman, grey hair—"

"Actually, it's black with streaks of grey." Fern clapped her hand over her mouth, a faint pinkness tinging her cheeks..

Glory studied the fairy suspiciously. "Fern, didn't you talk to him day before yesterday when he complimented your Key Lime Pie?"

"Oh, that Mr. Foster."

"Yeah, that Mr. Foster." Glory eyed Fern a moment, and then asked, "Fern, do you have a little crush on Mr. Foster?"

"Of course not." She started whipping whatever was in the ceramic bowl with a great deal of gusto.

"Really?"

"Fairy godmothers don't get crushes. They help find other people crushes." Fern stopped whipping and sighed.

"Maybe it would make them better fairies if they did experience a crush now and then."

"Maybe," Fern allowed. "But we've already pushed the fairy council as far as we dare. They're not going to let us change any more rules, and not getting crushes on mortals is a pretty big rule."

"But you wish things were different?" Glory pressed.

"I—"

Nick slammed into the kitchen. “We have a date.”

“Here, take this out to Mr. Foster while I talk to Nick.” Glory handed Fern the bowl of salad. “Oh, and take him a big glass of milk.”

“Okay.” Fern’s smile told Glory that although the fairy council might not believe in fairies having crushes on humans, Fern’s heart hadn’t been listening when the order came down.

“Glory?”

Glory stopped thinking about fairy crushes and looked at the man in front of her. Too bad things were the way they were. Nick Aaronson was...well, heck, he was gorgeous in a prim and proper, attorney-ish way. Glory would love to try to rumple his perfection. She’d love to run her fingers through his perfectly styled hair and muss it up. She’d like to take that tie and toss it, unbuttoning each of the buttons slowly, revealing the man underneath the suit. Then she’d—

“Glory?”

“Sorry. We’ve got a court date?”

He nodded toward the small office she’d set up behind the kitchen. “Let’s talk in there.”

She followed him into her office and jumped when she shut the door. She had been trying to avoid being alone with Nick and had managed it quite nicely. Yet here they were, alone behind a closed door. And there he stood totally unrumpled, just waiting for her to try to—

He slammed his briefcase onto her desk. “Two weeks. We’re before a judge I don’t know the slightest thing about. We have to plot a defense, but in order to do that, I need answers. I need you to help me this time. At that last meeting you just sat and watched the meeting fall apart. I need you, Glory.”

“You need me?”

“To help plot the fairies’ defense.”

Of course. He needed her for fairy help, not for rumpling help.

"Do you believe they're fairies?" she asked.

"Of course not. I've just fallen into the habit of referring to them as fairies, since that's how they refer to themselves." He paused and studied her a moment. "You don't believe they're fairies, do you?"

"Well, no. I mean, it would be nice to believe that there really is magic in the world, that happily-ever-afters really do exist, and that I'm about due for one." If she lived in that type of world, then Nick Aaronson might just be the man for her. They way he worried about the fairies, the way he'd taken this case to heart despite the fact he never wanted it in the first place, despite all the reasons she had for not falling for a man like Nick—if there really was magic in the world he'd be just the man for her.

But the fairies were simply delusional, harmless women, and Nick Aaronson wasn't the man for Glory Chambers. At least not in an ever-after sense. But maybe there was a slim chance he could be hers for a passing moment or two.

"Glory, you're a lovely woman, but I'm not ready for an until-death-do-us-part kind of relationship. I can hardly handle casual dating. I—"

Gently, she touched her index finger to his lips. "Shh. I wasn't asking you for a commitment. But maybe you should think about committing me after I do what I've been fantasizing about since you walked in the door."

"What?" he asked, his voice raw with something Glory knew should make her nervous, but instead made her more determined—

Before she could talk herself out of it, she kissed him. Oh, not some little light peck with her lips barely brushing his type of kiss. No, she kissed his socks off, kissed her own socks off, and wished she had the nerve to kiss off other articles of clothing.

There was a burst of recognition—a *this-is-where-I-belong* feeling—that terrified her, and conversely left her wanting more.

Tasting and exploring Nick, reveling in the fact he not only didn't end the kiss, but deepened it, exploring her as much as she was exploring him. Glory jerked his shirt from his waistband and slid her hands beneath the cloth, exploring the texture of the soft flesh covering his superb muscles.

Superb. Yes, that was an apt word to describe Nick Aaronson. Superbly male. Kissing him left Glory feeling totally feminine and totally—

She broke off the kiss. "We can't do that again." She withdrew her hand from beneath his shirt, took two hasty steps backward, and probably would have kept going except she backed right into the door.

"I mean it." Her voice was just a husky shadow of its normal self. "This can't keep happening. There are too many reasons why we shouldn't let it happen. Not the least of which is you and I really don't want to like each other."

"No, we don't, do we?"

"It's your family and their fairies that are doing it. If I believed in magic, I'd believe these feelings were just some spell." Actually, it would be easier to believe what she was feeling was someone else's will being imposed on her own. She'd never felt like this before. "So let's agree we'll work together for Myrtle, Fern and Blossom—with no more kissing. And when the case is settled go our separate ways."

"Deal."

Nick sounded relieved. Well, that was good because Glory was very relieved to know that soon her association with him would end.

But first they had to clear the fairies.

"So where do we begin?" she asked.

***

"So, let's start at the beginning," Nick said.

They were all back in his conference room, and he was bound and determined to finally get some straight answers from his pseudo-fairy clients.

In unison the three women started talking.

"We—"

"Grace—"

"In the beginning—"

"Stop!" Nick said. "Myrtle. You start."

The redheaded leader of the pack sat a little straighter and shot her sisters a pleased smile. "Fine. Once upon a time there was a writer named Grace—"

"We've been over this. Start at the beginning of this case, not at the beginning of Grace's life." Nick resisted the urge to scream. If he felt like screaming when they'd just started, how would he feel an hour from now?

"If you keep interrupting I'll never get the story told," Myrtle scolded.

"Fine." He felt his teeth clench and consciously relaxed them. "Go on."

"Grace wrote about love, but didn't have a love of her own. In her books she found loves for Nettie, Pauline, Susan, Alice, and the Spring sisters, April, May and June. But she couldn't find one for herself. So we came to help."

"And you're claiming you three are characters that Grace wrote about?" Nick asked.

"That's right. Did you ever read the *Velveteen Rabbit,* by Margery Williams? In it, the Skin Horse explains that toys that are loved long enough and hard enough become real. Well, Grace and her readers loved us hard enough and well enough that, like that rabbit, we became real."

"And you expect a judge to buy that?" Nick wasn't buying it, and from the look on Glory's face, neither was she. So how on earth could they expect a judge to? Actually, strutting a story like this could get an attorney in trouble, and Nick had no idea what kind of patience Judge Bernard Fallon had.

Fern shrugged. "It doesn't matter if he buys our story. It's the truth—that's all that matters."

"Max and Joy will testify for us," Blossom said.

"No." He wasn't about to tell them his brother and sister had not only offered to testify, but were insisting on it. "I have read Grace's books." Admitting that much was probably too much. "And while I'll admit the three of you resemble her characters, even if I believed in fairy tales, you couldn't be Grace's fairy godmothers since both Glory and I are sitting here looking at you. Grace's fairies could only be seen by their godchildren. You claim I'm the godchild, and yet Glory and an entire restaurant of customers can see you."

"Oh that." Blossom looked worried.

"Yeah, that," Nick said.

"Well, we went in front of the fairy council and got some rules changed," Myrtle said.

"Just like that, they changed the rules?" Glory jumped in.

Nick shot her a grateful look, then wished he hadn't looked at her. She was a distraction. Her coppery curls were piled into a wild mass on top of her head. And those blue eyes—he could get lost in their depths if he'd give himself half a chance. But he wasn't about to give himself that chance. Then he thought about the kiss they'd shared. The *kisses.*

He gave his head a shake. No. Giving Glory and her kisses even the slightest chance wasn't a good idea. And he certainly wasn't going to even consider thinking about what kind of woman would hire fairies, and then stand by them so steadfastly when they were in trouble. That type of loyalty and devotion were far more appealing than her kisses, which were far too appealing for Nick's own good.

"There were extenuating circumstances," Myrtle mumbled.

"Which were?" Nick pressed.

"We can't say." Myrtle's tone left no room for arguments. The fairies might muddle things, but they didn't intimidate easily.

"Blossom, can you say?" Glory asked.

The blonde ignored her sisters' distressed expressions and said in one rushed breath, "Oh, we had to argue long and hard, you know, and finally the council agreed there was no other way since Ber—"

"Blossom!" Myrtle and Fern yelled in unison.

"Sorry."

"Prove it to me," Nick said suddenly, hoping to catch them off guard.

"Prove what?" Myrtle asked.

"Prove that you're fairies." When they couldn't do magic, they'd have to admit they were delusional, and admitting there was a problem was the first step in solving it. Max would surely know someone who would be able to treat the three women's fairy delusions. Nick didn't know why he hadn't thought about it before.

"Do something magical." He tossed the gauntlet on the table and waited.

"We can't," Blossom said sadly. "I know it would make it easier for the two of you to believe, but we can't prove we're fairies by using our magic. It was part of the deal."

"What deal?" Glory asked.

"With the council. We gave up our powers...well, not really gave them up. We agreed not to use them in front of any humans, until these two cases—yours and Nick's, and Fiona's—are over."

"Grace threatened to make us mortal, and the council thought living like humans might be a humbling experience," Fern explained. "Nick, your dream was our last bit of fairy magic."

"Well, there was a few small things, but we never did them when any mortals were around," Blossom added.

"Yet, you claim to read minds," Nick stated more than asked.

"Oh, that's not magic," Myrtle said with a small laugh. "It's...well, for us it's a sense, like smelling or hearing or—"

"I get the picture." Damn. Every time he thought they were making headway, he found he hadn't moved an inch. "Back to your story."

Myrtle folded her arms and leaned back in her chair. "We fixed up Max and Grace, and did a bunch of little matches before we fixed up Joy and Gabriel."

"And that just left you," Fern said to Nick.

"The last Aaronson on our list." Blossom sighed, a breathy little Southern-belle-type sigh, and pressed her clasped hands over her heart. "It's so romantic. A whole family of happily-ever-afters, just like the Spring sisters."

Nick didn't want to hear any more fairy talk of happily-ever-afters with Glory. He didn't want to think about Glory at all. Glory who was once again just sitting across from him, taking in the conversation but not helping him. Blossom was prattling on about the Spring sisters, a group of Grace's fairy godmother romance books, but Nick was only half listening. He was concentrating on Glory. She was giving the small blonde her full attention, smiling a soft little smile as she listened.

Nick imagined what it would be like to have that attention focused on him, to have that soft smile all to himself. To have those soft lips pressed against his, opening and inviting him in. God, he wanted her. And the wanting seemed to grow by leaps and bounds, despite his need to keep his distance.

He realized that Blossom was winding down. "And then May built a small shelter on her lonely island and dreamed about Julian, while he was on his lonely island dreaming about her. Of course, we helped those dreams along."

"Of course it was your fault that they ended up on different deserted islands." Fern looked smug.

"Was not. You know it was you who suggest we strand them—"

"On the same deserted island."

"Girls," Myrtle scolded, then turned her attention back to Nick. "Oh, we've had some tough cases in the past. Why, I wasn't sure we'd ever get June out of jail for kidnapping."

Fern hurriedly added, "And then there was the time when

Susan had mono—"

Blossom interrupted. "And Cap fell and broke his hip."

"Or—"

Nick massaged his aching temples. He couldn't seem to keep his fairy clients—or his wayward thoughts about Glory—under control. "I think we get the picture. Those relationships turned out all right, but what I need to know is what happened to Fiona."

"And so did Max and Grace's, and Gabriel and Joy's relationships," Myrtle pointed out.

"But Fiona's romance didn't. What happened to Fiona?" Nick repeated.

"Her case might not have worked out *yet,* but May and Julian had a bit of a wait on their separate islands before they got their happily-ever-afters," Myrtle said.

"You mean you're not done with her?" Oh, God. That's all he needed. Three old ladies, convinced they were fairies, being sued and still trying to play matchmakers.

"Of course we're not done with her," Myrtle assured him.

Nick suppressed a groan. "So why are you here tormenting—"

"Nick, we're not tormenting you." Blossom looked hurt.

"—me if you're still working on Fiona's case," he finished, ignoring Blossom.

"Because Fiona's case is special," Fern said.

"And it's tied to yours," Blossom said, hurt feelings obviously forgotten.

"I thought you wanted Glory and me to get together." Fiona? Now they were going to try to fix him up with Fiona? That's all he needed—representing three fairy godmothers who were convinced he should fall in love with the woman suing them. He looked across the table at Glory—Fiona couldn't hold a candle to her.

Why had the fairies given up on giving him a happily-ever-after with Glory?

As if she really could read his mind, Fern said, "We haven't given up on you and Glory."

"Then how can I be tied to Fiona?"

"Oh, you're not tied to her romantically," Blossom said merrily. "Oh, tying. Now there's a thought girls. We could tie—"

"No tying," Glory warned. She'd been trying to keep quiet, but it was hard. When the fairies had said that Nick and Fiona were tied...well, she couldn't quite identify the feeling that had struck her chest like a physical blow. The feeling should have been relief, but it wasn't. No, relief in her case wasn't spelled F-I-O-N-A.

Deciding that since she'd entered the fracas, she might as get her two cents in, Glory continued, "No tying, and no matchmaking. We're here today because Nick has to have some sort of defense for you. We're not here so the three of you can get into more trouble."

Blossom wrung her hands together. "But Glory, we need Nick to get her and..."

"Get her who and do what?" Nick demanded, suspiciously.

Fern and Blossom opened their mouths as if they were going to answer him, but Myrtle squelched them with a look. "Now, Nick, we can't tell all our secrets."

Nick raked his hand through his dark hair, mussing it. Glory felt the urge to walk around the table and smooth it back into place for him. Instead of allowing the impulse—the silly impulse—to guide her, she sat on her hands.

Nick smoothed his hair back into place, saving Glory the trouble. "Listen," his voice was tight and controlled. "I didn't want to take this case, but I did because for some crazy reason I felt responsible for you all."

"We've answered everything you've asked," Myrtle said.

"Except for what happened between the three of you and Fiona," Glory pointed out.

"We visited her and had a plan, but she wouldn't cooperate," Blossom said. "If she'd simply listened, then she wouldn't have had to sue us."

"What plan?" Nick asked.

"We wanted her to come with us to Fairyland," Blossom said despite the fact Myrtle was shooting her looks that could kill. "And it's against the rules to just kidnap people."

Finding the weak link, Nick pressed, "But according to Grace, you had her kidnapped."

"Oh, we didn't kidnap her, Clarence did," Blossom said. Myrtle looked like she was going to shush her, but Blossom shook her head and said, "He needs to know the truth. We couldn't just take Fiona to Fairyland if she didn't want to go. If you'd read your fairy tales, you'd know that people have to enter the fairy-circles of their own free will."

"Oh, we might try to trick them, but they ultimately make the decision," Fern added.

Myrtle thumped a fist on the table. "Your mouths waddle like a duck's a—"

"Myrtle!" Fern and Blossom gasped in unison.

"Why do you want Fiona to go to Fairyland?" Glory asked, trying to diffuse the situation and get this meeting back on track.

"Why, haven't you guessed?" Fern and Blossom asked together, despite the fact Myrtle's face was a brighter shade of red than her hair.

"How could we guess anything?" Nick roared. "Just answer the question. Why do you want Fiona to go Fairyland to find her own happily-ever-after."

"Why, Nick, Fiona's a fairy," Blossom and Fern said.

"She doesn't know she's a fairy," Blossom added. "But she is."

Myrtle jumped out of her chair and stalked from the conference room.

"Oh, now she's going to be in a snit," Fern moaned. "Myrtle

likes to think she's the boss, but you two needed to know what's going on."

"Come on, Fern, let's go see if we can catch up to her and talk her out of being mad."

Fern and Blossom scrambled out of their seats and out of the room.

Glory stared at Nick, feeling at a loss. How did she comfort a man who represented three supposed fairy godmothers who were being sued by another supposed fairy who apparently didn't know she was a fairy? The first thought that came to mind was kissing. Lots and lots of kissing.

Nick stood and started gathering his papers. "That's it. I quit."

"Nick, you can't quit." Glory wasn't sure what to do. She didn't believe the fairies, but she also didn't believe they intentionally harmed Fiona. She didn't believe they were a danger to anyone but themselves. And, she realized, she didn't believe Nick was going to quit.

"Well, I do." He stalked toward the door.

She rose and simply touched his elbow. It was enough to stop him. "But if the case is coming before the judge so soon, what will we do?" she asked softly.

"How should I know? And you don't have to do anything, you're not being sued."

He shook his arm as if to free himself of her touch, but Glory held on. She wasn't going to let go of Nick that easily. Not that she wanted him for anything more than his legal expertise. "I may not be the one being sued, but I am responsible for them."

"Why? Supposedly they're my fairy godmothers, not yours."

"But they work for me. And I believe they have their hearts in the right place."

"Do fairies have hearts?" he sneered.

"You can't just walk away from this." She was talking

about the fairies, she assured herself even as she moved closer to him. She took his papers and gently placed them on the table. "You can't just walk out on us."

"I can and I am." There was little conviction in his voice. "Glory, I can't do this."

"Please?"

Nick stopped, as if that one word had frozen him. And as he stood, frozen in place like a male counterpart of Sleeping Beauty, Glory did what she'd been fantasizing about. She kissed him. Her hand no longer grasped his elbow. No, somehow it and its mate had twined themselves around Nick's neck, pulling him closer.

Kissing him was as addictive as it was intoxicating. She couldn't get close enough. She wanted more. Without meaning to, she tugged the back of his shirt out of his pants and began to explore his body. Her hands ran up and down his bare back, memorizing the feel of him, his every contour. And still it wasn't enough. She wanted—

Glory realized just what she wanted, and it scared the hell out of her. Slowly she withdrew, moving away from Nick and trying to put space between all the things she'd like to do to him...with him.

"Glory." Her name wasn't a question, but a statement of confusion. Confusion that echoed her own.

"Nick. I need you to represent the fairies. I honestly believe you're the only one to do the job. But that has nothing to do with that kiss."

"Then what was the kiss about?"

"I want you. I don't want to want you, but there it is. And as sweet as your kisses can be, that's not all I want."

"What else do you want, Glory?"

"What I'd really like to do is strip you naked and have you, here and now. I'd like to remove your clothes, one piece at a time, and lay you on that table. Then, still fully clothed, I'd like to memorize your body. I'd like to touch it and taste it until you couldn't stand another minute of it. You'd sit up and rip my clothes from me, leaving me bare and exposed and then we'd..."

"Finish it, Glory. Don't leave me hanging."

"And then we'd make love. But we can't do that."

"Why not?"

"Because if just kissing you can make me feel so alive—so wanton—what would happen to me if we made love? I'd never be the same. I'd need you, and I can't feel that way again. I needed someone once upon a time, and then he wasn't there. It hurt, Nick. It hurt so damned bad. I needed him, I trusted him, and he not only betrayed that trust, but showed me in the cruelest way that he didn't need me."

Glory realized what she'd confessed and thought she'd die of mortification. Straightening, she looked Nick in the eye. "I'm not going to open myself up to that kind of vulnerability again, especially not with a man who's made it clear he doesn't want to want me, either. I need you, but only as an attorney. Are you going to walk out on us, Nick?"

She stood there, all her wounds exposed to him as if she was daring him to hurt her again, to prove to her that all men where like the one who'd hurt her. Nick wanted to find her ex-husband and beat him bloody. He wanted it in a savage, uncivilized way. And conversely, he wanted to sweep Glory gently into his arms and comfort her. He wanted to kiss her and whisper that he would never hurt her. But never hurting her meant not getting involved with her.

The vulnerability he saw in her only proved how wrong getting involved with Glory Chambers would be. His family accused him of only dating shallow women. Maybe they were right. But he couldn't hurt a shallow woman. He could hurt Glory. And that was the one thing he didn't want to ever do.

He admired so many things about her. The way she'd rebuilt her life according to her terms and the way she defended the fairies were a large part of that attraction. She was a caring and giving woman. Her ex-husband was a fool for letting her go.

Nick was a fool as well to allow an association with her to continue. The more he was around Glory Chambers, the more he fell under her spell.

He should tell her in no uncertain terms to find someone else. He should put as much distance between them as possible. Instead, he found himself saying, "I'm in. I'll probably get disbarred for blatant stupidity, but I'm in."

"They can't disbar you for being stupid, or else half the attorneys in the US wouldn't be practicing." For a moment Glory looked as if she was going to hug him. But then the wall was once again erected between them, and the glimpse of her innerself she'd allowed him faded. She simply shot him a social smile of thanks. A look she could have given a stranger.

It wasn't a look a woman would give a man she'd kissed. At that small social smile Nick's temper flared. "We should talk about what just happened."

"What just happened is you agreed to represent the fairies."

"No, before that. I want you too, Glory. But—"

"Nick, I'm a big girl, and I realize that despite the chemistry that we seem to have, getting involved with each other would be stupid. So, let's both admit we want each other, but there's this great big BUT there, looming like an undefeatable hurdle."

"Listen, you don't want to be hurt again. I can understand that. I don't want to be hurt ever. I look at my mom and dad, at Max and Grace, and at Joy and Gabriel. How often can those types of relationships happen? They do say three times is a charm. They've all been trying to set me up forever it seems, and I'll be honest, some of the women were tempting, but not tempting in a trip-to-the-altar sort of way, if you know what I mean. I want a relationship like the rest of my family has, and I'll be honest enough to admit I don't know that I'll ever find it. And if I can't have what they have, I don't want anything."

He paused. "Does that make sense?"

She nodded. "Unfortunately, it does. Maybe we should just acknowledge that we are attracted to each other and then move past it."

"Can we?"

"I think we're both adult enough to handle the attraction and not let it get in the way of the business at hand."

"Fairy godmothers," he said with a resigned sigh. He obviously was stuck with fairy godmothers, and with an ever-growing attraction for Glory Chambers—an attraction he wasn't going to pursue.

"Right, three meddling, slightly crazy, but good-hearted fairy godmothers," Glory said.

"I don't have much confidence in winning this case."

"That doesn't matter, since I have enough for both of us."

"Would it be breaking our newfound rules if I admitted that I like you, Glory Chambers? Like you a lot."

Glory smiled, and for a moment that wall she was desperately trying to cling to slipped. "No. And as long as we're both laying our hearts on the table, I'll admit I like you as well. You may be an arrogant, occasionally annoying attorney, but I like you anyway. Maybe if we'd met at some other time, maybe..." Her voice trailed off.

"Yeah, maybe."

She firmly held onto her resolve. She wasn't going to fall for Nick, no matter what the fairies said. "But we didn't meet somewhere else. We're here, and we've got fairies to take care of."

"Right, fairies." He followed her to the office door. "And Glory?"

She turned. "Hm?"

"Part of me wishes I was looking..."

"Me too," she admitted.

"Okay, let's get ready for the judge. It's going to take

whatever magic the fairies possess to help us win this one." He stopped and corrected himself. "It's going to take more than magic. It's going to take a miracle."

Seven

Nick watched the judge walk into the room and stared at him in surprise. He was a retired judge? Judge Bernard Fallon didn't look much older than Nick himself. Nick couldn't help wondering what kind of judge he was. The more sympathetic the better, at least from the fairies' standpoint.

Nick had needed more than two short weeks to prepare. He'd interviewed Max, Grace, Joy and Gabriel, and he had four rather sane sounding character witnesses. But though they might sound like rational human beings, how rational could they be if they were on the stand testifying that they believed in fairies?

He glanced at Glory, sitting directly behind the fairies. She gave him an encouraging nod.

It was going to take more than encouragement to win this case. He glanced at Bill Richards and the willowy brunette he was representing. He'd interviewed Fiona as well, and he wasn't quite sure what to make of the woman who'd cast them all into this insane situation. She seemed so sincere and didn't come off the least bit crazy. But believing three middle-aged women could bring her a happily-ever-after true-love was crazy.

"Please be seated," the bailiff said.

Though he was young, the judge was an imposing presence. He cleared his throat. "Before we get started, I have a couple of things I need to get out of the way. First, anyone familiar with the courthouse realizes that I'm just filling in here. This is my first time sitting an Erie bench, and I have to say I am not impressed with the nature of this case. Frivolous law suits take up precious court time, and this suit is frivolous. No one, Miss," he checked the paper in front of him, "Fayette, has the power to make you happy—no one except you yourself. And suing three old ladies—"

"I object," Blossom hollered.

The judge shot her a glare that would have cowed a much braver man than Nick. "Pardon?" he asked, his voice full of menace.

"I said, I object to being called old, Your Honor." She gave a little curtsy. "We all know that the three of us aren't the oldest people in this room."

"Blossom," Nick hissed.

"Counsel, I suggest you warn your client against any further outbursts, or I will be tempted to hold you in contempt." The expression on the Judge's face left no room for doubt that he'd follow through on his threat.

"Me?"

"Yes, you. Control those three." He paused. "Now, where was I? Oh, happiness. As I was saying, it is up to every individual to secure his or her own happiness. The question as I see it isn't whether or not Ms. Fayette is happy, but whether the three women in question are responsible for her unhappiness because they purposely misled her.

"As I said, I don't want to waste my time or the court's time on frivolous lawsuits. I don't plan on dragging this on forever. I don't have much patience."

Fern raised her hand. "Pardon me, Your Honor, you don't have *any* patience."

"Counselor?" A dark eyebrow rose, and in that one word Nick could hear his cell door locking with a click.

"Would you three be quiet before I get tossed in jail for contempt," he whispered at his clients, even as he wished he could yell at them.

"But, Nick, you really can't let him talk to you that way," Fern said. "Next thing you know, Bernie will be—"

"Fern," Nick warned.

"Fine, I'll shut up. But mark my word you'll be sorry if you let Judge Bernie start playing despot this early in the trial."

"Counselors, did you both try to work out some settlement between your clients?"

"Yes, Your Honor," both Nick and Bill Richards said in unison.

"And I take it the four women couldn't find any middle ground."

"My client wouldn't settle," Bill said. "She doesn't want money. She wants her happily-ever-after."

Judge Fallon frowned. "And as I said, the court can't grant her that. Only she can find her own happiness."

"Your Honor, may I speak?" Fiona asked softly.

"That's what you have counsel for, Ms. Fayette. To speak for you." He paused. "But I tend to be less formal than most judges you'll meet. I run my court to suit myself—"

"He runs everything to suit himself," Myrtle mumbled.

The judge shot her a nasty glare that indicated he'd heard her, but continued speaking. "—and it would suit me to hear what you have to say for yourself."

The tall, slender woman stood. "I know this case seems frivolous to everyone. If Mr. Richards hadn't known my father, there's no way he would have taken my case."

Bill Richards started to object, but Fiona held up her hand, silencing him, and continued, "You know it's true, Bill, and I can't really blame you. I know this entire case seems silly. It appears that I'm just a lonely woman who believed in fairy tales, and is amusing herself at the court's expense. That's how it might look, Your Honor, but that's not it at all."

"So, tell us, Ms. Fayette, how is it?"

"All my life I've had everything anyone should want. I

had parents who adored me, who would have laid the world at my feet if they could have. And don't get me wrong, I loved them, too. But I didn't fit in. I excelled at school, but I always felt there was more to know, some big secret that no one was letting me in on. There's this hole in the center of my being, and it's growing bigger every day. I'm afraid it will totally engulf me some day.

"And then these three women came to me. They said they knew how I felt. They understood that having everything didn't mean anything if you didn't feel complete. They said they understood and could make it better. They promised me a happily-ever-after, and I want that."

She paused a moment, as if gathering her thoughts. "That hole? I think it's the other piece of me that's been missing since birth. I think it's the man I'm destined to love. They swore they knew who he was and that they would bring him to me. That's what I want. I don't want money, and I don't want them punished. I just want my happily-ever-after. I know it sounds crazy, but I think they know where that piece of me is. I want him. I want to belong to someone.

"So, I realize this lawsuit seems frivolous to you, but it's everything to me." She sat, and the entire courtroom was silent.

After several minutes, the judge straightened his collar and cleared his throat. "Thank you, Ms. Fayette for clearing that up. The court still maintains your happiness is your own responsibility, but it will hear your case.

"Now, Counselors, both of you have requested a closed court and no jury due to the...sensitive nature of this case. I was going to refuse, but after listening to Ms. Fayette, I agree that we should avoid exposing her personal affairs to the public. This will be a closed court. I don't want anyone involved with this case talking to the press. I will not have my courtroom turned into a media circus, and I guarantee fairies and happily-ever-afters would be a three-ring circus. I will hear this case and make the decision based on the facts as they are presented to me.

"Mr. Richards, you will begin tomorrow at eight o'clock. This court is adjourned." The judge banged his gavel.

"All rise," said the bailiff.

Judge Bernard Fallon stalked out of the room.

"So what does that all mean?" Fern asked.

"Tomorrow we start." Nick glanced at the woman suing the fairies. She was leaving the courtroom with Bill. He felt a stab of sympathy for her but quickly buried it. He couldn't afford to sympathize with Fiona Fayette. He had her fairy godmothers to look out for.

If anyone deserved some sympathy, he did.

***

"I want to call my first witness. Fiona Fayette," Bill Richards said bright and early the next morning.

The slender woman made her way to the witness stand and was sworn in.

Bill lounged against the prosecution table. "Ms. Fayette, yesterday you touched briefly on the circumstances that have brought us here. Let's start at the beginning. Could you please tell us how you met the defendants?"

"I was at work when they approached me." Nick noted that Fiona's pale skin was all but translucent today, and the stab of pity he felt yesterday reasserted itself. "Later I saw them at Bloomingdales, on a plane, and in my apartment. But I was the only one who could see them, even when I wasn't alone. They said that only their godchildren could see them, but now everyone can. I don't understand that."

"For the record, where do you work? Bill asked.

"The Herb House." Fiona's voice was little more than a whisper. "We provide natural health and beauty products."

"And tell us about that first meeting with the defendants." Bill's voice echoed the concern Nick felt. This woman appeared to be close to the edge of her ability to cope.

"I was alone in the store when suddenly Myrtle, Fern and

Blossom were there. They startled me."

"Do customers usually startle you?"

"No." She shook her head. "But I was in the back room working on some paperwork because there were no customers in the store. We have a buzzer on the door to let us know when someone comes in, but it didn't buzz, and they were just there, standing in front of me and grinning."

"Do you see these women in the courtroom?" Bill asked.

"There." She pointed a trembling finger at the fairies, naming each. "Myrtle, Fern and Blossom."

"What did you do then?" Bill asked.

She tore her eyes away from the fairies and looked at Bill. "I just assumed I hadn't heard the buzzer, and I asked them if I could help them. They said no, but they could help me."

"And did they tell you how they planned to help you?"

"They told me they were fairies and had come to help me find my own happily-ever-after." Fiona's voice grew even softer.

Gently, the judge said, "Ms. Fayette, you'll have to speak up."

"I'm sorry." Louder this time, she said, "I said, they promised me my own happily-ever-after."

"And you wanted that happily-ever-after?" Bill asked.

"Doesn't everyone?"

"Let me ask you, Ms. Fayette. Are you happy?"

There was a pregnant pause, as if Fiona was weighing the texture of her emotions. "No, sir, I'm not."

"The prosecution rests."

Nick eyed the witness. She looked as if she could drop at a moment's notice. Quickly he glanced at the judge, trying to gauge his reaction to the testimony. Yes, he was sympathetic, despite his proclamation yesterday about not caring for frivolous lawsuits. Nick would have to tread carefully. He didn't want to seem as if he was attacking the obviously fragile witness and thereby alienate the judge.

Slowly, he approached the witness stand. "Ms. Fayette, are you going to tell the court that you believe my clients are fairy godmothers?"

"That's what they said," she affirmed.

"That's not what I asked," he pressed, his voice as soft and soothing as he could make it. "I asked if you believed them when they said they were fairies."

"No," she answered slowly. "Not at first."

"So what convinced you?"

Here was a question Nick really wanted answered. His entire family believed in the fairies, even Gabriel and Max, who claimed to have never seen the fairies until they met them at Glory's place. What could convince four rational adults, and now Fiona, to believe in fairies? Nick hoped she could do a better job of explaining than Max, Grace, Nick and Joy had done.

"Like I said, they appeared to me in public places, and I was the only one who saw them. That was pretty convincing. And..."

"And?" Nick pressed.

"Well, they knew things," she said.

"What kind of things?"

She shifted nervously in her seat. "Things about me. Personal things."

"A good detective could find out many personal things about you, but that wouldn't make him a fairy godmother," Nick pointed out.

"They knew things that no private detective could find out. Things I dreamed about. Things I wished for. They read my mind. And, yes, after a time I did believe that they were fairies."

Mentioning dreams made Nick uncomfortable. He had a mental image of Blossom sitting on his lap, but he quickly shut it off. He didn't need to be reminded that the first time he'd met the fairies was in his on-its-way-to-becoming- x-rated dream.

A little more forceful, Nick said, "So three fairy godmothers burst into your life and promise you your dreams will all come true. I'm willing to concede that they are, as you believe, fairies."

"What?" asked the Judge.

"Oh, Nick, we knew you'd believe us," Blossom said.

Nick turned and faced the fairies. Glory was sitting right behind them, an incredulous look on her face. Nick hadn't discussed this strategy with any of them. He simply smiled what he hoped was an encouraging smile. "I didn't say I believed my clients were fairies. I believe they're harmless romantics. But for the purposes of this trial, I'm willing to concede the possibility that they are truly fairies."

"In which case I want my happily-ever-after," Fiona said. "They promised me my own-true-love."

Nick moved directly in front of Fiona. There was a splash of color lighting her cheeks for the first time. "Miss Fayette, when the fairies promised you a happily-ever-after did they give you a timetable?"

Fiona looked startled by the question. "Pardon?"

"Did they tell you when this happily-ever-after would begin?" he pressed.

"No," she answered hesitantly.

"Did they ask you to do anything specific to help bring about this happily-ever-after?" he asked. Fiona remained silent.

Nick turned to Judge Fallon. "Your Honor, please instruct the witness to answer the question."

"Ms. Fayette, this is a reasonable question," the judge said. "Would you please answer it."

"They asked me to go to Fairyland with them," Fiona admitted softly.

"What?" Judge Bernard Fallon roared.

Louder this time, Fiona repeated, "I said, Myrtle, Fern,

and Blossom asked me to go with them to Fairyland."

The judge pounded his gavel. "I want to see Myrtle, Fern and Blossom alone in my chambers. Now!"

"Nick, he can't do that, can he?" Eternally merry Blossom had turned decidedly un-merry.

"Your Honor, this is highly unusual," Nick said.

"This entire case is highly unusual, Counselor. Myrtle, Fern and Blossom—my chambers now. Court is in recess." The Judge struck his gavel and stood.

The bailiff said, "All rise."

The room rose and, as the Judge stalked out of the courtroom, Nick returned to his table.

"Nick, he can't make us go, can he?" Fern asked.

"He's the judge. He pretty much rules this courtroom."

"That's always been Bernie's problem. He's always the boss," Fern muttered.

"Well, if we have to go face him, we're taking you and Glory with us." Myrtle looked grim.

"I'm your attorney, he can't keep me out. But he certainly isn't about to let Glory in."

"Just let him try to keep me out," Glory said. She patted the obviously shaken Blossom's shoulder.

The admiration Nick had for Glory's defense of the fairies rose another notch. He found himself taking her hand and giving it a quick squeeze. He wasn't sure if he was offering her moral support or seeking it for himself. He'd had his share of strange clients in the past, but these three were the oddest.

The five of them slowly followed the judge into his chamber behind the courtroom.

The Judge de-cloaked, then sat at his desk. Pointing at Nick and Glory, he said, "You two—out."

"I'm sorry, Your Honor, but I'm their attorney and I must insist that I stay." Nick could see that his answer didn't please the judge. But pleased or not, the judge couldn't legally force Nick to abandon his clients.

"And I'm their employer, and they've asked me to be here." Glory stood defiantly, as if she was daring the judge to try to remove her.

Admiration didn't quite cover what he felt seeing her so willing to fight for the fairies. Something in Nick's chest leaped. She was beautiful, standing arms akimbo, daring the judge to kick her out. If he needed her, would she defend him with this kind of passion? Nick suddenly realized that he wanted her passion.

"Both of you can stay, but you're to sit there and not make a sound." The Judge pointed to a couch. "You three, front and center." The three fairies hesitantly obeyed.

"So, your Glory and Nick are banding together on your behalf, but that doesn't mean they're in love."

"That doesn't mean they're not, Bernie," Fern said, flippantly.

Nick cringed. No one called a judge such a familiar name, especially when it was obvious he'd like nothing better than to throw them in a cell and a toss away the key.

"That's Judge Bernie," the judge said, running his fingers through his hair in apparent frustration. "At least for now."

"Ha. For now? You've always been of the opinion it's your job to sit in judgement over everyone else. You're condescending, egotistical and..." Blossom paused.

"Yes," the judge urged softly.

Too softly for Nick's peace of mind. He jumped to Blossom's defense. "I think what my client is trying to say—"

"I think I told you to sit back there and be quiet," Judge Bernie barked.

"But—"

"Nick." Glory took his hand and pulled him back onto the couch. "I don't think he's fooling around."

"You're obviously a very intelligent young lady." The judge gave Glory an encouraging nod. "Sit, young man."

"Who is he calling young? He's not much older than I

am," Nick muttered to Glory. "I don't know how he can be a Senior Judge."

"Did you have something you wanted to share with all of us, Mr. Aaronson?" Judge Bernie asked, sounding more like a school teacher than a judge.

"I'd love to—"

Myrtle cut him off. "Nick, let us handle Bernie." She turned to the judge. "This is all your fault, and you know it. That's what you're so mad about."

"You still haven't given me any proof," the judge maintained.

"We've given you enough that you should have at least investigated it," Myrtle argued.

"Speaking of investigating," said Nick, "I think we need to talk about how it is you know my clients, Your Honor. Maybe we should investigate your recusing yourself from this case."

"That's not going to happen because your clients don't object to my hearing this case. Do you?" he asked, Myrtle, Fern and Blossom.

"Sorry, Nick," said Myrtle. "It's a good point, but we need Bernie to hear this case. No one else will do."

The judge nodded. "They're convinced I need to be here, and there's nothing either of us can do to change their minds." To the fairies he said, "But I still need proof."

"Proof of what?" Glory asked.

"Proof that Fiona's a fairy," Blossom said. "Though Bernie here would like to believe we're lying, now that he's met her, he knows it's true. And even though he doesn't want to admit it, he knows what he has to do."

"I'm the judge here." The judge suddenly didn't look quite so confident. "I don't have to do anything."

"And would you like to explain to Nick and Glory how many cases—human cases—you've ever heard?" Fern asked innocently.

"The three of you are treading on dangerous ground. I deserve—and I insist on—a certain amount of respect. My position has earned me that much."

"What you deserve is a good spanking." Fern said. "Everyone in Fairyland talks about how your mother indulged you and spoiled you."

"One more word about my mother, and I'll . . ."

"You'll what?" Myrtle said, drawing herself up to her full four and a half feet.

Judge Bernie pointed at Glory and Nick. "I'll hold them in contempt."

"Wait a minute, we haven't done anything," Glory protested. "You told Nick to shut up and sit here, and that's just what we're doing, so how can we possibly be in contempt?"

"That's it. The two of you are in contempt." The Judge stood and pushed his chair back with such force it thwacked against the wall. He stalked to the door and slammed it open.

"Judge!" Nick protested.

"Bailiff," Judge Bernie called. "Find these two a cell. "

"You've got to be kidding," Nick yelled.

"Bernie, you can't put them in a jail with criminals," Blossom said. "If you try, I'm calling Berrybelle myself and telling her what you're doing."

The imposing, self-righteous judge suddenly looked a little cowed. "You wouldn't."

"Oh, I would," Blossom promised.

"They're in contempt."

"No, I'm in contempt," Myrtle corrected him. "I'm in total contempt of a man who is such a coward he won't meet his destiny head-on. And since I've known you all of my life, I have to admit I can't believe you're this much of a coward."

"How dare you!" Judge Bernie snarled.

"Easily," Myrtle said. "We used to be friends, Bernie. You were only a couple classes ahead of us in school. I hate to see what you've become. You won't even consider the possibility you're wrong. And I dare you to try to put these two in jail. They wouldn't be there long."

"You wouldn't," he growled.

"Watch me," Myrtle said.

"And me," echoed Fern.

"And me, too," Blossom added.

Myrtle's hands were on her hips. "We both know who would win."

"But—"

"Let them stay here for the night," Blossom offered softly. "In your office. They have a bathroom, and there are no criminals, at least not after hours."

"You know you can make sure they don't leave," Fern added.

"The three of you are supposed to be on our side!" Glory hollered.

"We are on your side, silly. We're keeping you out of jail," Blossom said.

"But you're convincing him to lock us up here, rather than to drop this absurd contempt charge." Nick couldn't believe what was happening. Just a few weeks ago he was a normal, slightly dissatisfied attorney. The only thing he was looking for was a case he could care about, not a case like this—a case with women who thought they were fairies, plaintiffs who agreed, and a judge who was as mad as the March Hare.

Nick felt as if he'd dropped down Alice's rabbit hole and was beginning to wonder if he'd ever find his way out.

"This entire situation is absurd," Nick muttered.

"Absurd?" Bernie echoed, the word obviously not sitting well.

Nick didn't give a damn what Judge Bernie felt. The man was a nut-case. This entire case was crazy, and everyone connected to it was as well, including his brother, sister and their spouses.

"Now, don't go getting upset, Bernie," Fern said placatingly. "Nick's having a hard time accepting the way things are."

"I'm not accepting this any better than he is," Bernie said.

"But you will," Blossom promised. "Now that you've met Fiona, how can you not?"

"The three of you are insane," Bernie muttered.

"Finally, you've said something that makes sense," Nick growled.

"If we are insane, you'll have to blame Grace," Blossom said. "Now, about Nick and Glory."

"Fine." Judge Bernie looked as if he'd reached the edge of his rope and was hanging on by just a strand. He stood in front of Nick and Glory. "You two are in contempt, and I sentence you to spend the night in here. When I come in tomorrow, I expect an apology."

"For what?" Glory asked.

"You can figure that out tonight. You'll have plenty of time. Now sit there and let me finish." He turned his attention to the fairies. "What's this about the three of you inviting Fiona into Fairyland? You know the rules."

"You know what they say about the mountain coming to Mohammed," Myrtle said with a finger waggle. "And it wouldn't have broken any rules. We told you, she's a fairy."

"Half fairy," Bernie corrected.

"Any hint of fairy blood is enough, and you of all people know that, Bernie." There was disappointment in Myrtle's tone.

"How dare you bring that up?" Bernie gasped.

"The fact that Berrybelle loved a mortal and gave him a son isn't anything to be embarrassed by. The fact that you're behaving like an ass is." Myrtle shook her head in apparent disgust.

"Bernie, you disappoint me. You disappoint all of us." Fern shook her head as well.

"The two of you are making this worse," Blossom, the for-once-in-her-life-voice-of- reason, said. "Bernie needs time to adjust. You're trying to railroad him into his destiny instead of allowing him to discover it on his own. Remember Terry. You allowed him to discover Pauline wasn't a Paul, and that she was in fact the love of his life."

"Of course the poor boy spent weeks worrying about his sexual orientation because he was so attracted to Paul, never knowing *Paul* was a Pauline." Fern let out a little laugh that didn't sound very sympathetic.

"I'm done. We'll continue this in court tomorrow. I'm not going to be reprimanded by some egotistical coward." Myrtle started toward the door. "You'd better leave these two something for dinner, and Blossom, make sure they have clean clothes for the morning."

"Thanks, Nick," Blossom said as she trailed after Myrtle. "You did a great job today."

"You're really not leaving us here," Glory said in disbelief.

"I may not be able to control Myrtle, Fern and Blossom, but here I'm the judge and you're in contempt." There wasn't an ounce of sympathy in Judge Bernie's voice.

"I'm not an attorney. Why am I here?" Glory pressed.

"If it weren't for the two of you, I wouldn't be here going through this absurd charade. You've annoyed me. Deal with it." Bernie started toward the door. "Dinner will be delivered at six. The phone and the door won't work. Have a great night."

Glory watched helplessly as the fairies and the judge left. She could hear them continue to argue their way down the hall. She turned and faced her incompetent attorney. "Now look what you've done."

"What I've done?" Nick looked incredulous.

"Yes, what you've done. We're in contempt and locked in this room for the night."

"Don't worry. This man is obviously nuts. I'll call the

president judge and have him straighten this all out." Nick strode to the office phone and picked it up. "I can't believe it. He was right. It's dead."

"What do you mean, it's dead?" Glory felt a sense of panic begin to build. She didn't want to be locked up for the night, especially with Nick Aaronson. Nick, who left her feeling weak and feminine. Nick, who left her tongue-tied. Nick, who made her feel like a frizzy-redheaded school girl once again, unsure of what to say and what to do.

No, Glory did not want to spend a night locked up with Nick Aaronson.

And conversely, Glory wanted to spend a night with Nick Aaronson. And that wanting was why she absolutely, positively didn't want to spend a night with him. She had plans that didn't include a fling with a handsome attorney whose entire family believed in fairy tale happily-ever-afters.

Once upon a time, Glory believed in them, too, but that time was long past.

"There's no dial tone. It's not working." Nick slammed the receiver down.

"You're an attorney. Certainly you have a cell phone." Glory had to get out of the office and away from the attorney who had her fantasizing about briefs, and not the legal kind. No, as he paced in the courtroom today she'd fantasized about what kind of briefs he wore. Boxers? Silk? Flannel?

"Hang on." Nick opened his briefcase. "We're in business." He held up a cell phone triumphantly, then flipped the phone open and punched in a number. "Nothing."

"What do you mean, nothing?" Glory felt as if all the oxygen had been sucked from the room. Carbon dioxide poisoning was the only explanation for her wild thoughts. Thoughts that included sweeping the clutter off the insane judge's desk and having her way with Nick. Her wicked, wild way with him.

"Glory, are you all right?"

"Am I all right?" Her mind full of images of what she'd

like to do to Nick, Glory nodded, thankful attorneys couldn't read minds like supposed fairies could.

"Are you going to ask what I mean about everything I say?"

Glory forced herself to dismiss the x-rated images cluttering her mind and nodded. "Yes. At least until you make sense. What did you mean when you said nothing."

"I meant, nothing, as in there is no power to this phone." He tossed the cell phone back into his briefcase.

"Don't you charge your phone?"

"Yes. I just took it off the charger this morning."

"Then it should work." Forget the briefs. Glory wanted Nick totally briefless. She wanted him completely naked, and the wanting was growing by leaps and bounds with each passing minute.

"Yes, it should work." He ran his fingers through his hair in frustration.

Glory wanted to smooth his hair, and then she wanted to continue smoothing her way down his whole body.

"But it won't work," she said, no longer talking about cell phones, but of the temptation of starting a relationship with Nick, though he didn't know that.

"No. It won't work."

She sighed and tried to ignore her fantasies. They'd both admitted a relationship, even a purely physical one, wouldn't work.

"So now what?" she asked.

"It's only four o'clock. The building is still full of people. We'll just hammer on the door until someone gets help. Unless you have a better plan." He watched her expectantly.

Since she had decided against her let's-get-naked-plan, Glory shook her head. "Unfortunately, I don't."

He pressed his ear to the door. "I hear someone."

She pounded. "Help." After a minute with no response, she listened again and pounded some more. "They're either ignoring us, or they can't hear us."

"They have to hear us." Nick swore and pounded the door one last time.

"Maybe the judge warned people off. He's mean enough to do something like that." Glory did not like the mean judge. Didn't like him at all.

"Glory, we might as well face it. We're here for the night." Nick fell back onto the couch, slumped in defeat.

"If the fairies really are fairies, maybe they'll rescue us." Or, maybe this was exactly what they wanted. Nick and Glory trapped together for the night. She was pretty sure that the idea would appeal to their matchmaking-itis.

"Are you kidding? They'll be delighted to have us stuck here together all night," Nick said, echoing her thoughts.

"So now what?"

"I guess we get comfortable and wait."

Nick sat at the judge's desk and Glory curled up on his couch, glad to have as much space as possible separating them. He turned and looked out the window, creating further illusions of separation.

Glory's erratic thoughts were disturbing. She tried to analyze them, but got nowhere. Every thought about Nick led to thoughts about a Naked Nick, which led to thoughts about everything the fairies had said, which led to...

"Nick?"

He turned back toward her. "What?"

"Do you believe in fairies?" she asked, though that wasn't what she'd planned to say. She wasn't sure what she'd planned to say, but asking if Nick Aaronson believed in fairies wasn't it.

"I—"

"Because I am starting to," she blurted out.

"You can't be serious."

"I am." There she'd said it. She'd admitted that Glory Chambers, who until a few months ago was a corporate exec making decisions that affected thousand of people's lives, believed in fairies...well, almost believed. Whenever she looked at Nick and her heart gave that funny little flutter, she could believe that almost anything was possible, even three meddling match-makers being fairy godmothers.

"How can a reasonable, rational woman believe in fairies?" he asked.

"Your sister and brother believe in fairies, and from what I can tell, they're reasonable and rational people."

He shook his head in disgust and raked a hand through his dark hair, messing it up some more. "I used to think so. But then they both fell head over heels in love and, obviously, as they fell they lost some of their rationality."

"Nick?"

"What?"

"I'm starting to believe the fairies were right for another reason, too." She got off the couch and started toward the desk and him.

"What's the other reason?" he asked softly.

"When they said you were my own-true-love—"

"You're not in love with me." It wasn't a question, but a statement.

"No," Glory admitted. "I'm not. But I think the fairies were onto something."

"What?" He rose and backed away from her advance.

"I'm in lust with you." She had lusted before. Once upon a time she'd lusted over Garth, but eventually the lust had died along with the marriage. A casualty of Cynthia's double D bra. What she'd had with Garth hadn't been love. It was just a case of lust, and that's all this was with Nick. She needed to believe that.

He continued backing up and appeared to be trying to process what she'd said.

"What did you say?" he finally asked.

"I'm very, very in lust with you."

"Glory." There was a warning in his voice.

Whether he was warning her to stop this conversation, or warning her what might happen if they kept talking of lust, she wasn't sure. But she continued. "I want you. I don't want marriage, and I certainly don't believe in happily-ever-afters, but I do want you, Nick."

"Glory." This time there was more of a groan in his voice, and maybe a hint of weakening.

"I gave up on happily-ever-afters when I walked away from my old life. A happily-ever-after can never depend on another person. It's up to each individual to find their happiness on their own. That's about the only thing Judge Bernie and I agree on. And I'm doing that. I have Glory's Chambers—I own it and run it my way. I don't answer to anyone. That makes me happy, and if that happiness dims, I'll simply move on." She moved closer, and this time, Nick didn't counter her steps but stood still against the far wall, simply watching her.

"And I want you," she said, her husky voice almost unrecognizable to her own ear. "I'm in lust with you. Satisfying that lust would make me happy. For now, at least, it would make me very happy."

"Do you know what you're saying?" he croaked.

"Yes. When I left my husband the divorce was ugly. I decided then and there I didn't like attorneys, but I was wrong. I like you a lot. And I want you." She stood right in front of him, sandwiching him between her body and the wall.

"Glory, this doesn't make sense."

"It doesn't have to. I'm not asking for any promises. We're here, and it looks like we're not going anywhere tonight. Rather than sit here and worry, I'd like to put our night to better use." Slowly she reached out, spanning the distance between them, and traced his jawline with her index finger.

The slight touch made Nick's body react. His head might be saying this was a mistake, but his body didn't appear to agree.

"I..." Nick paused. He should say no. Since he'd dreamed about the fairies, his life had been a nightmare. Fairy godmothers, redheads who haunted his days and nights. Representing fairies. And Glory, standing here gloriously offering him what he'd been wanting since he'd met her. "I'm not sure this is a good idea."

"I am," she whispered. Just that one fingertip was touching him. It moved down his neck and softly traced the hollow of his collar bone.

"Glory."

Down his chest, she traced, slowly reaching his waist. She unbuckled his belt. "You're probably right. This isn't a good idea." She unsnapped the pants and slowly drew the zipper down.

"If it's not a good idea, what are you doing?"

"I think sometimes we get so caught up in analyzing every little nuance of our lives that we miss out on living our lives. I'm tired of missing out." Glory smiled. "Nick. What if the fairies are right? What if there is something happening between us?"

This might be wrong, but it felt so right. Nick didn't have any defenses against what he wanted...he wanted Glory more than he'd ever wanted anything.

"Have I ever mentioned I have a thing for redheads?" he asked.

"Really?" Glory began unbuttoning his shirt. "And despite the fact I'm not overly fond of attorneys, I guess you've figured out that I have a thing for one attorney."

"And you think we should explore whatever it is between us?" Finally, as if admitting his desire had unlocked something, Nick allowed himself to touch her. He ran his hand through her unruly curls. Glory leaned into him, and he welcomed the feel of her.

"I think that makes sense, Counselor."

"Isn't it convenient that Judge Bernie has that great big

overstuffed couch?" He pulled her toward it, shedding his jacket on the way, and lowered her onto it.

"Very convenient," she murmured as she unbuttoned his shirt.

Nick ran a hand up her thigh beneath her dress, then paused. "Glory, if we do this, I don't want you to regret it in the morning."

"If we don't do this, I'll regret that in the morning." She placed her hand on his and led it higher. She groaned.

"Do you know how much I've wanted to do this all day?" he asked even as his lips descended to meet hers.

"No, but show me how much," she suggested. Touching Nick was explosive. Glory wanted to go on touching him. She wanted to meld into him until there was no Glory and no Nick, just a mixture of the two of them. She wanted him.

Holding him, touching him, kissing him...it felt right. It felt like coming home.

"You're sure?" he asked one last time.

Making love to Nick Aaronson might be a mistake, but Glory was sure that even if it was she was going to do this. She was going to spend this one night in Nick's arms. She was done analyzing, done playing it safe. This night—this one night—she was going to let her heart lead her.

And it was leading her to Nick Aaronson.

That was enough for now.

"Yes," she finally answered. "I'm sure."

What clothing remained between them disappeared as if by magic.

Magic. The moment was magic, and the moments that followed as well.

The seconds lasted minutes, minutes stretched into hours. Time lost all meaning. They touched, they memorized. Glory was lost in a sensuous haze of her own making. No. Of their making. Nick made her feel truly beautiful and desirable, things she didn't think she'd ever feel again.

"Nick," she whispered, unsure what else to say. Sure that there were no words to express everything she was feeling.

The emotions overwhelmed her, as much as the feel of Nick's body pressed to hers overwhelmed. She couldn't sort out all the emotions, and she didn't want to. She just wanted simply the release that was tantalizingly at hand.

"Nick," she whispered again, pulling him closer with rising urgency.

"Tell me what you want," came his hoarse reply.

"I want everything. I want you."

Glory's words were all the invitation Nick needed. He sampled her, tasting, touching. He was teasing her, driving her to the edge—driving himself there as well.

"Glory," he moaned when the feelings grew to the point of no return. "I need you."

"Now," she whispered.

That one word was all the invitation he needed. He buried himself within her, and at that moment of intimate connection Nick knew his entire world had shifted. How, he wasn't sure, but as they moved in a rhythm as old as the ages, he knew that nothing would ever be the same. Because of this woman. Because of Glory.

Her orgasm sent him spiraling into his own, and he lost himself in a thousand explosive pieces. For how long, he couldn't know, but as he drew back from the small piece of heaven, he immediately felt the loss.

"You're so quiet," Glory whispered.

Nick searched for something to say. He wanted to tell her how deeply their moment together had affected him, but the words wouldn't come. How could he explain to Glory what he didn't understand himself?

But finally he asked, "No regrets?"

She snuggled against him. "No regrets."

"You're sure?"

Glory sensed he needed assurances as much as she did.

She reached out and lightly ran a finger down his jawline. There were so many words she wanted to say, but none would come. So finally she settled on simply, “I’m sure.”

Later, maybe she’d sort out these feelings and share them with him. But for now, she just lay back and basked in the feel of this man in this one magical, timeless moment.

Eight

"I'm sure," Glory said again.

"But how could we have missed them?"

They were still cuddled on the couch, both staring at the tray sitting on the coffee table. The huge tray contained what appeared to be enough food to feed a small dinner party, not two adults.

The tray wasn't the problem.

The fact that neither of them had noticed anyone putting it there was.

The fact that if someone had indeed come into the room, they'd done so while Glory and Nick were engaged in the most glorious experience Glory had ever experienced.

The fact that someone had come and gone, and they had missed the opportunity to get word to the outside world that they were locked in a madman's office was. A second thought hit her. If someone had been in the office that person knew what she and Nick had done.

Despite the fact she was well beyond the age of consent, Glory felt heat rush to her cheeks.

"I swear, I didn't see anyone," she said again. "Who do you suppose it was? Because as amazing as it was—"

"It was amazing," Nick agreed with something that sounded like smugness.

"—I can't imagine I'd miss someone walking into the room carrying that huge tray and setting it down half a foot from where you and I were..." she paused.

She was inclined to say, *having sex,* but that didn't go nearly far enough. What she'd done with Nick wasn't merely sex. But to say *making love,* well, that was too scary. She didn't want to make love with him because that might imply she loved him, and Glory Chambers most certainly didn't want to love Nick Aaronson.

She liked him. When she'd gone to his office and asked him to take the fairy case, she'd never doubted, despite his blustering, that he'd refuse her. She trusted him. She liked and trusted Nick, and she'd liked to...well whatever she'd called what they'd just done, she'd like to do it again. But she didn't want to love him.

Nick shook his head. "No one was in this room, Glory."

"You're sure?"

"Yes."

"So—"

"How did the tray get here?" he finished for her.

"Nick, before we...well, you know. Before I said I thought they could be fairies. Do you think..." she let the question trail off.

"I don't know what to think anymore." Slowly he traced her bare arm from shoulder to wrist. "I do know one thing, though."

"What?" she asked, the sparks of desire flaming into passion.

"Dinner can wait a while."

"How long a while?" She reached for him.

"As long as we need it to."

***

Later, both of them wrapped in the judge's afghan, they ate their meal.

"It's still hot." Glory said, around a mouthful of the best lasagne she'd ever eaten. "How can it still be hot?"

"I don't know." Nick glared at his lasagne, as if it was the Italian dish's fault that it was still hot.

"Yes, you do. You just don't want to admit it."

Fairies. Nick Aaronson—a logical man who spent his life dealing with facts—had fairy godmothers. Three fairy godmothers. Three fairies who were being sued by another half-fairy, and the judge hearing the case was a half-fairy as well.

Glory was damned right. He didn't want to admit it.

"Oh, stop glaring at it and eat it," she said. "The food's not to blame."

Nick shoved a bite of the delicious pasta into his mouth. Glory was right. It wasn't the lasagne's fault. But whose fault was it then? He glanced at the naked redhead next to him, and despite his annoyance, smiled. She looked as if she'd just spent the late afternoon and the better part of the early evening making love. The look was good on her.

It was a look Nick hoped she'd keep the remainder of the night. Making love to Glory was addictive. He wanted nothing more than to throw her back onto the couch and continue memorizing her body.

"Don't look at me like that," she said.

"Like what?" he asked.

"You know like what. When you look at me that way, I..."

"You what?" he asked.

"I want you again. I mean, we've already...well, you know, twice."

"You know?" he asked with a small laugh.

Her fork paused midway between the plate and her mouth. *"You know* is the best I can come up with. The term sex sounds just too crude, and though it's an accurate term, I don't want to use it. And I'm not ready to say we were making love."

"Why the hell not?" He slammed his plate onto the table.

"Why the hell not what?" she fired back.

"Why the hell can't you say we were making love?" He

wanted to grab her and shake her. What they'd done together wasn't just sex. Hell, Nick knew all about just sex, and what he'd done with Glory didn't even come close.

"Because you don't love me, Nick," she said softly. "And I don't love you."

"You're sure?"

"Aren't you?"

Was he? There was something between them, something Nick had never experienced before. Was he ready to call that something love?

"I don't know what to think," he finally answered.

"That's what I'm saying. A few short weeks ago I thought I had my life mapped out. I had a new business that was all mine. I had a plan. And a man wasn't part of that plan. I'd had enough of men."

"But?" he prompted.

"But then three women showed up in my restaurant, and all those plans fell apart. Now, I'm sitting here naked, eating lasagne with a man—an attorney no less—and I don't have a clue what I feel or what I think. There's only one thing I know."

"What's that?"

"That whatever we want to call what we just did—"

"Twice," he felt the need to point out.

"Twice," she agreed with a smile. "Whatever you call it, I'd like to try for a third time, and then I'd like to spend the rest of my night wrapped in your arms. I don't want to try to analyze this, and I don't want to talk about fairies and happily-ever-afters."

"I think that's one wish I can make come true without any fairy-help."

And Nick found that sometimes wishes could come true without any fairy-magic.

***

Eight o'clock the next morning they sat waiting on the couch dressed in clothes that had mysteriously replaced yesterday's wardrobe. They'd eaten a breakfast that had magically appeared and were savoring their second cups of coffee.

"So how are we going to handle today?" Glory asked.

"First off what happened here—"

"Is no one's business but ours," she finished.

"Right."

"About the trial?"

"I don't have a clue. Part of me thinks I should just leave the fairies to their own devices. That's what they did to us yesterday."

"But oh, what devices they were." She reached out and laid her hand on his arm, relishing that mere touch. Despite all the unanswered questions, despite the fact that she had no idea where whatever-they-called-it with Nick would lead, she was deliriously happy.

Happy.

Glory couldn't remember the last time she would have used that word to describe herself. When she worked for Michaelson's she was content, even satisfied. When she was married to Garth she was...

Well, whatever she was, it wasn't happy. Somewhere along the line her marriage to Garth had simply become a part of her life. Like having a left hand. She never really thought about it, never really invested herself in it. It just was.

Maybe he'd felt the same way, and that's why he had strayed with Cynthia's double D's.

She glanced at the dark-haired, brooding man sitting next to her.

Rational, logical Glory Chambers was sitting next to a man she'd spent a wild night being pleasured by. She'd been held in contempt of court. She'd employed three fairies who were being sued. And she honest-to-pete couldn't remember the last time she'd felt so good.

She was totally, utterly happy.

"They should be here soon," Nick muttered.

"Yes, they should," she agreed.

"I want this done today."

As happy as she felt, if looks counted for anything, Nick wasn't feeling nearly as good. She withdrew her hand. "You think you can wrap up the trial today?"

"Yes," was his flat response.

She itched to reach out and touch him, to soothe whatever deep, dark thoughts he was having. She wished, just this once, she had the fairies' ability to read minds. What was he thinking, sitting there staring into space? Was he regretting last night? She wished she could ask him, but she couldn't find the words. Just as she couldn't find a way to span the distance between them and touch him.

Finally, to fill the quiet space surrounding them, she said, "I'm sure the fairies will be relieved to have this behind them."

"What about you?" he asked, his tone rough.

"What about me what?"

"Do you want this to be behind you?"

"Are we talking about the trial, the fairies, or something else?" Was he saying he wanted to put last night behind them and forget it? Was he asking her to do the same? She didn't think she could forget last night, and what's more she didn't want to.

"I'm talking—"

She would never know what Nick was talking about because at that second the door to the office burst open.

"Well, you two don't look the worse for wear," Blossom chirruped merrily. She breezed into the room wearing a dress of a particularly violent shade of yellow. It flowed around her, whipping against her ankles as she walked in.

"Actually, they look a bit better," Fern said. She was wearing a moss green pantsuit with a little brown mushroom pattern.

"So, how are you handling things today?" Myrtle asked,

trailing the other two into the room. Her bright red jumpsuit would have looked more at home on someone in their teens than on a middle-aged fairy.

"Oh, you don't like it?" Myrtle glanced down and sighed. "Fine." The jumpsuit disappeared and was replaced by a rust-red pantsuit. "Better?"

"How did you..." Glory let the question trail off because she already knew the answer. "You're fairies."

"Well, it took you long enough to admit it," Blossom said. "And what about you, Nick? Do you believe we're fairies?"

"I'm an attorney. I don't have to believe anything. I just have to defend you."

"Nick." Glory felt a stab of sympathy for him. He hadn't asked to be thrust into this absurd situation. But her sympathy rapidly turned to annoyance. Neither had she.

"Don't *Nick* me. I don't have to believe. I don't want to believe. I won't believe. But I will defend." He stood. "That will have to be enough for all of you."

"I suppose it will," Fern said.

Myrtle shook her head and simply sighed. "Fine. Right now we have a trial to get ready for. Bernie said he wants us all to clear out of his office and be ready and waiting in the courtroom in ten minutes."

"That suits me just fine," Nick said. He stood and stomped out of the room.

"He's not happy," Blossom whispered sadly as he left.

Glory looked at the three fairies and then at the doorway Nick had gone through. No, he didn't look happy. Then she smiled. Nick might not be happy, but she was.

She might not want to define the reason, but she would admit, at least to herself, that despite the fact Nick was an annoying male and an attorney to boot, she was very, very happy.

"He'll come around soon enough," Fern said.

"Is that a promise, or just wishful thinking?" Glory asked.

"We're fairies. All our thinking is wishful," Fern said.

"I guess that's good enough for me."

***

"Please be seated," the bailiff said.

"So?" Judge Bernie said, looking at Nick and Glory.

"So what, Your Honor?" Nick returned, though he knew what the Judge wanted. An apology. For what, Nick still hadn't figured out.

"I believe you and Miss Chambers have something to say to me." Judge Bernie steepled his fingers beneath his chin and eyed Nick expectantly.

He stood. He'd had enough fairy-nonsense, and more than enough crazy judge nonsense. "Sure. I have a lot to say about you—"

Glory sprang to her feet and cut him off. "We're sorry, Your Honor, sir."

"For what, precisely?" the judge asked.

"For annoying you?" she asked more than stated.

"Oh, I can think of a couple more things I'd like to add," Nick started. The three fairies all shushed him as Glory grabbed his shoulders and forced him back into his seat.

"What's he going to do, turn me into a toad?" Nick grumbled.

"Maybe. He turned Partywinkle into a firefly when he was ten. Berrybelle spent a week trying to undo the spell," Fern whispered.

"Pardon?" Judge Bernie said loudly. "Is there a problem, Counselor?"

Nick looked stubborn and started to say, "Yes. There is—"

Glory cut him off again, almost shouting over him, "No, Your Honor. We're very sorry for annoying you."

"See to it you don't annoy me today," Bernie barked. "You may be seated."

Glory sat.

Nick turned around and whispered in her ear. "You didn't have to apologize."

"Nick, I'm pretty sure it's best not to annoy judges. Or fairies," she whispered. "And since Bernie is supposedly both, I think it's wise to avoid annoying him. And though I'm sure you'd make a cute firefly, I think you're cuter just the way you are."

"You can't seriously believe that he's a fairy, or that Fern, Myrtle and Blossom are either, for that matter."

Glory had worked for an international company. She was a woman who dealt with facts. A down-to-earth woman. Despite some of the odd things that had been happening lately, she couldn't honestly believe in fairy godmothers. But she did.

She nodded. "And don't forget, Fiona's half-fairy."

"But—"

"Mr. Aaronson, am I to take your silence as a sign you do not wish to continue cross-examining the witness," Judge Bernie called.

Nick swung around and faced the bench. "Yes, Your Honor. I mean, no, Your Honor. I definitely have a few more things to ask Miss Fayette."

"One warning, Counselor. You're annoying me again. So unless you want to spend another night in my office, I'd tread carefully."

Recalling just what had gone on in the judge's chambers last night, Nick wasn't so sure it would be a bad thing. He forced the image of Glory smiling beneath him out of his mind and followed Fiona to the witness stand.

Judge Bernie said, "And may I remind you, Miss Fayette, that you're still under oath."

"I remember, sir," she said softly.

Nick stared at the tall, willowy lady. She did have an unearthly air about her, but unlike Glory, he wasn't about to admit she was a fairy. But if the court admitted that she was, then maybe he had a way out for Myrtle, Fern and Blossom, he realized.

Nick suddenly had a plan of attack. It was crazy, but this entire situation was crazy, so maybe crazy was just what they needed.

"Miss Fayette, could you tell the court about your childhood?" he asked.

"What about my childhood?" She seemed startled by the question.

"Were you happy?"

Slowly, Fiona nodded. "I had a very normal childhood, Mr. Aaronson. My parents loved me. I loved them. I played with dolls and read everything I could get my hands on. I lacked for nothing."

Bill had mentioned that Fiona had always felt alienated, as if she didn't belong. She'd as much as admitted her alienation yesterday, but that's not what she'd just said. Nick needed more than a surface commentary on her childhood. "And in school, did you fit in?"

"I..." Fiona was extremely fair complected, but her face lost all color and appeared almost translucent.

"Yes?" he pressed softly.

"I didn't quite fit in," she said, her soft voice almost a whisper.

"You didn't fit in." He repeated and then appeared to mull it over. "Would you tell the court why you don't feel as if you fit in at school?"

"I object," Bill said. "The witness isn't a psychologist, and therefore isn't able to answer the question of whether or not she was well-adjusted in school."

"No," Nick said easily. "She's not a psychiatrist. But since she's answering to her own mental state, I think the court can allow that Miss Fayette is an expert, even without an M.D. behind her name."

"I'll allow it," Judge Bernie said. "But, as I said, tread

carefully, Counselor. You don't want to annoy me."

"I'll bear that in mind, Your Honor." He turned his attention back to Fiona. "Why didn't you fit in, Miss Fayette?"

"Things were always happening. People noticed and were uncomfortable around me."

"What kind of things?"

"Odd things."

Nick sighed. Getting an answer out of Fiona Fayette was like pulling teeth. "Such as? Could you give the court some examples?"

She was silent a moment, but finally answered, "I heard voices—people whispering, even when no one said anything. It was almost as if I was hearing their thoughts. Sometimes I responded to what they were saying—at least when I was younger, I did. But eventually I learned it wasn't worth it."

"Why?"

Fiona suddenly sat a bit straighter. "I really don't see how that has bearing on this case," she said with more force.

"I think it does," Nick disagreed. "Your Honor?"

Judge Bernie was peering down at the witness stand. "I believe Mr. Aaronson might be right in this instance. Answer the question, Miss Fayette."

"People tend to think you're odd if you answer questions they never asked. The voices I heard were people's minds whispering—their surface thoughts."

Nick nodded. A woman who read minds made about as much sense to him as the rest of this crazy case. "You read minds?"

She shook her head. "I couldn't really read someone's deep inner thoughts, but sometimes I knew things...things no one told me. Eventually I learned not to listen." She paused with a look of concentration on her face. "But if I concentrate, I can still hear those voices. Yours is saying this is all crazy."

"That's a pretty good guess that anyone connected with this case might be thinking."

"And if I go a little deeper, I can hear you worrying about what to do about Glory." She paused. "She was amazing last night, but you're not comfortable thinking about taking the relationship any further. You almost wish the judge would hold you in contempt again because then you'd have an excuse to be with her again, but you wouldn't have to make any commitment."

"I object!" Nick hollered.

"So do I!" Glory yelled.

"It was your question, Counselor," the Judge said. "You can't object just because you don't like the answer. But if Ms. Fayette is right, I might object to the two of you carrying on on my couch."

"If you hadn't been an ass and held us there over night, it would never have happened," Nick said. "Making love to Glory wasn't something I planned on doing."

Making love to Glory was a mistake. Rather than diminish his need, last night had only intensified it. And that intensity was so raw, so big, that Nick was at a loss as to what to do about it.

"It wasn't making love," Glory argued.

Nick turned around and glared at her. "Well, it sure as hell wasn't just sex." That was the scariest thing of all. What he and Glory had done last night was more than anything he'd ever experienced before. More than anything he'd ever thought to experience. He needed time to figure out just what it was, and what the hell he was going to do about it.

"If it wasn't sex, Nick, what was it?" Blossom cried.

"That is none of your business," Nick snapped. "This entire case is insane."

"No. Wanting to forget about last night is insane. But this case is almost over, isn't it Bernie?" Myrtle asked. "I can't imagine what more you need to hear."

"I'm not willing to admit you're right about the happily-ever-after," the judge said. "But, I think I've heard enough to make a decision."

"But we haven't called any of our witnesses," Nick protested. "You can't make a decision without hearing our defense."

"Sit down, Counselor," Bernie snapped. "And you, Ms. Fayette, you may take your seat as well."

Judge Bernie shuffled some papers on his desk as the courtroom settled back down. His reluctance was apparent as he began. "When Myrtle, Fern and Blossom came to me and said they'd found the love of my life, well, I was a bit skeptical, given what I know of them."

"Now, Bernie, have we ever been wrong?" Myrtle asked.

Rather than snapping at her for interrupting, Bernie merely sighed. "No. Never wrong, though I hate to admit it. But the three of you have a hell of a way of making matches."

Myrtle sprang to her feet. "But Bernie—"

"Sit down and let me finish."

Myrtle sat and Bernie continued. "Ms. Fayette, when the three defendants first came to me about you, I didn't believe them. No, I take that back. I didn't want to believe them. So I chose not to. They went to the council and petitioned for a change in the rules. When the counsel granted it—over my objections—I was more than a bit put out. That made me even less inclined to listen to them. I was stubborn."

"He's always been a stubborn one," Blossom said. "Berrybelle used to go half out of her mind over some of his scrapes. Why, there was a full three years he refused to use his fairy powers at all. The trouble he got into—why it was even worse than some of the scrapes Myrtle, Fern and I have gotten into. There was the time—"

"Blossom!" Myrtle hollered. "Bernie's talking."

"Thank you, Myrtle," Bernie said.

"No problem, Bernie."

"Oh, I'm sorry," Blossom said, sinking lower in her chair.

"Where was I?" Bernie asked.

"You were being stubborn," Fern said.

"Yes, so I was. And it turns out you were just as stubborn, Fiona." It was the first time the judge had called the plaintiff anything but Ms. Fayette. Her name rolled off his lips like a caress. Nick was sure if he noticed it the rest of the courtroom did as well. He glanced at his fairy clients. They were all practically swooning.

Bernie didn't seem to notice. "When Myrtle, Fern and Blossom came to you and invited you to Fairyland—"

"I'm not a fairy," Fiona protested.

"No you're not," he said gently. "You're half-fairy. So am I. And, Fiona, when they promised you a happily-ever-after, I was the one they were referring to. We don't know each other, but there's obviously a common heritage that we share. And maybe, if you'd be open to getting to know me, we'd find that Myrtle, Fern and Blossom—no matter how unconventional their methods are—are right. Maybe we're exactly what each other has been looking for."

He paused a moment. "I'm going to dismiss this case, and then I'm going to invite you to come with me to Fairyland."

"And if I feel as if I don't belong in Fairyland, either?" she asked.

Nick suddenly had a burst of insight that didn't rely on mind reading. Fiona was afraid to take this step because, if it was wrong, and she didn't find her happily-ever-after in Fairyland, maybe she'd never find it. Maybe she'd never fit in anywhere.

A little voice in the back of his mind whispered its empathy with the feeling, but Nick pushed it back, trying to ignore it.

Bernie must have sensed her fear because he answered softly, "Then I promise I'll help you find where you do belong. But Fiona, I have a feeling that's one promise I won't have to keep."

He stood, once again stern and in control. "Court is dismissed." He motioned to Fiona, and they both disappeared through the door behind the judge's bench and into his chambers.

Nick stood as well and looked at his clients. "Well, that's it then, Ladies. You're off the hook."

"Thank you, Nick. You saved us." Blossom flung herself into his arms and hugged him fiercely. Myrtle and Fern followed suit.

"You're a great attorney," Fern said. "We'll definitely recommend you to all our friends."

"Your fairy friends?" Nick asked.

Three heads—a redhead, a blonde and a brunette—bobbed up and down.

"Would you mind terribly if I decline the offer? Representing the three of you was all the fairy work I plan to do."

"Ah, Nick?" called Bill Richards. He was standing by his table looking confused. "Do you want to explain what just happened here?"

"Do you really want me to try, Bill?" Nick countered.

Bill snapped his briefcase shut. "No, I don't think I do. I'm going to find the nearest bar and try to obliterate the memory of this entire case. Care to join me for a drink?"

Nick finally glanced at Glory. Yes, he needed a drink. A whole bunch of drinks. Maybe if he drank enough he could figure out just what he was going to do with the redhead he'd spent the night with.

"Yes, Bill, I believe I'd like that drink." He snapped his briefcase shut, picked it up and hurried after Bill. He needed to get away from fairies, away from happily-ever-afters, and away from Glory. He needed time and some distance to figure out just what he felt for her, to figure out what he was going to do about her—about them, if there was a them.

"Can we expect you to bill us, Counselor?" Glory called after him.

He pivoted and found himself face-to-face with redheaded

fury. A pang of guilt stabbed at him, but he ignored it. He'd never promised Glory anything. The fairies had said he was her Prince Charming, but Nick knew better. He was no prince, and he'd never been charming.

"What do you want from me?" he asked.

"What do you want from me?" she countered.

"The problem is, I don't know." Looking at her, Nick could think of one thing he wanted—to take Glory someplace quiet, someplace with no fairies, and then he wanted to make love to her again all night long.

"Call me when you do." She turned and started back toward the fairies.

"So that's it?" he asked.

She turned, facing him. Nick could see pain in her expression and longed to soothe her until that pain disappeared. But since he was the source of her pain, there wasn't anything he could do.

"Apparently it is," she said quietly.

Glory wanted to shout that this didn't have to be it, that the fairies had promised they could have so much more, but she didn't. She wasn't sure if she didn't say it because she was afraid Nick would reject her, or if she was afraid he'd say the fairies were right, and they could have a happily-ever-after. She didn't know what she wanted from him, so how could she expect him to know what he wanted from her?

"Goodbye, Glory," he said in a tone that spoke of finality.

"Goodbye, Nick," she whispered too soft for him to hear. So soft she wasn't even sure she'd spoken out loud. She watched the man of her dreams walk down the hall and turn the corner out of her life.

"Glory," Blossom said, gently placing her hand on Glory's shoulder.

Glory shrugged it off. "Don't worry, girls. You're batting one for two today. Fiona and Bernard will have their happily-ever-after. Fifty percent isn't bad odds."

"He might come around," Fern said.

"I don't think so." And that was fine. It wasn't as if she couldn't get by without Nick Aaronson. She'd proven to herself she didn't need anyone. She could make it on her own.

The problem was, she thought as she stared at the vacant hall, she didn't want to make it on her own without Nick. She wanted...

"What do you want, Glory," Myrtle asked softly.

"I want Nick," she said, finally admitting to herself her deepest desire. She didn't just want him for a night of making love—she finally gave what they'd done a name. No, she wanted all his nights and all his days. She wanted him, body and soul.

"Want Nick to what?" Blossom asked.

"To love me. I want what his family has—what Max and Grace, and Gabriel and Joy, and his parents have. I want a happily-ever-after."

"So?" Fern prodded.

"So what?" The three fairies were watching her expectantly, but Glory had no idea what they expected. She'd admitted she wanted Nick. They'd just have to admit he didn't want her.

"So what are you going to do about it?" Myrtle asked.

"What can I do? Nick doesn't love me, and you said you can't make people fall in love."

"That's right," Myrtle said sadly. "Though I've often thought it would be easier if we could."

"Whoever said love was easy?" Blossom asked.

Despite the fact her heart had just followed Nick out the door, Glory managed a little smile. "No one, I guess."

"That's right. Love isn't easy, even if you have fairy godmothers helping you out," Blossom said.

"I think love might even be a bit harder with fairy godmothers helping you out," Glory muttered.

"Say the words, Glory," Myrtle commanded.

"What words?"

"The words you wouldn't say to Nick." Blossom's hand was pressed to her chest, and she once again had a Southern belle swoon going.

"What good will it do me? Even if I say them to him, he doesn't feel the same way."

"Words carry magic of their own, especially that one word." Fern didn't look swoony. She looked slightly annoyed. "You know what you need to do. Say the words, Glory."

The three words she thought she'd never say again. Words she'd never fully understood until she'd met a certain dark-haired, infuriating attorney. "I love Nick."

She loved his sense of honor, honor that led him to defend the fairies. She loved his sense of family—his love for them all showed every time he talked about them. She loved...she just loved him. That love had nothing to do with fairies. But they were right, it did have a magic all its own.

"So, I ask again, what are you going to do about it?" Myrtle said.

"I don't have a clue." Obviously making love last night hadn't touched Nick like it had touched her. The trial was over, and he was done with the fairies and, apparently, done with her as well.

"You could make a wish," Fern said.

"The three of you are not my fairy godmothers."

"That's right, we're Nick's." Blossom looked exceedingly pleased with herself, and that alone made Glory nervous, but when the yellow fairy pressed, "But give it a try anyway."

"I wish I could make Nick love me."

"No, no, no," Fern scolded. "You can't make Nick love you any more than we can make him love you."

"So what is it I'm supposed to be wishing for?"

Sighing with disgust, Myrtle said, "Glory Chambers wishes for a chance to make Nick understand what he means to her, and what she feels for him."

Bernie blinked into the hall. He was about the size of her forearm and fluttering in the Erie Courthouse's hall on a pair of gossamer wings. "Is that what you wish?"

"I thought you were taking Fiona to Fairyland?" What was he doing here? Coming back to hold her in contempt again?

Bernie sighed. "I have taken Fiona home. Actually we were just starting dinner. So, if you don't mind hurrying this up."

Fiona, a very small fairy-version, blinked into sight next to him. "He's all mine as soon as he clears up this one last job. You want a chance with Nick, right?"

"Right. I'm not asking for you to make Nick love me, I know you can't. But I want a chance to tell him what I'm feeling."

"That's your wish?" Bernie asked.

"Yes." Glory might be scared, but she wasn't going to let fear stand in her way of a happily-ever-after. If she said nothing, she might not ever have Nick. And if she told him how she felt, he'd either realize he felt the same way and they'd live happily-ever-after, or he'd decide he didn't, and she'd learn to live without him. The odds were better with telling him.

"Come on, Bernie, take care of it," Fiona said. "I want to go home. There's so much to see and learn."

"Fine." Bernie reached out and took Fiona's hand, giving it an affectionate squeeze. Then he turned his attention on Glory. "It's done. You'll have your chance with Nick."

"How? When?" she asked.

"Tonight." And with that Bernie and Fiona disappeared into what Glory hoped was their very own happily-ever-after.

"Tonight," she echoed. Tonight she'd tell Nick Aaronson how she felt. Myrtle, Fern and Blossom had said those three words had a magic about them. Glory could only hope they contained enough magic to make Nick love her back.

Nine

"Ooh, la, la, what a handsome man you are, cheri," the winsome blonde whispered in his ear.

Nick Aaronson frowned as she caressed his cheek but continued the dialogue that had become part of the ritual, "And just think, I'm all yours for tonight...and for as many nights as you want."

"Oh, but Nicky, it's not me you want," Lola said as she disappeared.

In her place sat Blossom. But unlike the first time she interrupted this dream, she wasn't smiling indulgently at him. She was frowning even before Nick stood up in shock, dumping her from his lap.

"You know, this has got to stop." Blossom stood and rubbed her well-padded posterior.

"You're damn right. You've got to stay the hell out of my dreams." He glanced around the deserted French bistro, waiting expectantly. "Where are they?"

Fern and Myrtle appeared in a flash. All three were once again wearing their cancan outfits, Nick noted.

"Well, Gracey won't let us wear them around her," Fern said.

"Listen, just get out of my dreams." He'd spent the evening drinking with Bill. Neither of them had talked about fairies. They'd simply gotten pleasantly drunk and then taken cabs home.

Nick had fallen into bed, determined not to think about fairy godmothers, happily-ever-afters or Glory. Sleep had always been a refuge, this dream especially so.

Until now.

"Get out of my dreams," he said again.

"Not until you admit this isn't your dream," Blossom said cheerily.

"What the hell do you mean this isn't my dream? Of course it's my dream. I came here years ago and have dreamed about it since. This is my dream—this place and Lola are mine. They're where I go when I need to get away. And let me tell you, I came here to get away from you. So I want you out."

"No, you just relive this rendezvous with Lola and remember it at night," Fern said. "This isn't your dream. You've got to see that."

"You know what your dream is," Blossom said.

"Or rather *who* your dream is," Myrtle corrected.

"Listen, I defended you, but I don't believe in you." Nick Aaronson didn't need fairy godmothers. He didn't need anyone. What he needed was a good night's sleep.

"That's okay, Nick. We believe in you," Fern said.

"Listen, get out of my . . ." he paused, an image of a certain redhead flashing through his mind's eye. The fairies were right, though he'd never admit it. Lola had never been his dream.

"Of course we're right." Myrtle looked smug.

"Don't read my mind," he snapped.

"We wouldn't have to if you'd be honest out loud," she said.

"What exactly is your dream, Nick?" Fern asked innocently, as if she hadn't been reading his mind along with Myrtle.

"Just get out," he said. He needed time to figure out what to do about his newly identified dream. "Go."

"Not until you admit it," Fern said stubbornly.

"I don't have to admit anything."

"Oh, but you do, Counselor. You're under oath." said Judge Bernie.

Gone was the French bistro. Nick was sitting on the witness stand, and Bernie was once again on the bench. "You were asked a question, now answer it. And answer it truthfully."

"Could you repeat the question?" Nick asked.

"Just what is your dream?" Myrtle repeated.

"No, no, Myrtle you're wrong." Before Myrtle could protest, Fern said, "Just *who* is your dream, Nick."

"I want to take the fifth."

"You can't." Bernie thumped his gavel.

"I can on the grounds my answer might incriminate me."

Glory stood in front of the witness stand. "Bernie?" she said, ignoring Nick and turning instead to the fairy judge.

"Tell Nick what you said this afternoon," Bernie prompted.

"Oh, no. That wasn't my wish."

Suddenly, the entire courtroom, including Glory, heard her disembodied voice say, "I'm not asking for you to make Nick love me. I know you can't. But I want a chance to tell him what I'm feeling."

"So, here is your chance. Tell him what you're feeling," Bernie said. "I have to get home. Fiona's waiting."

"I love him. Okay?" She turned to Nick and faced him angrily. "I love you, and I don't know why. I mean, you're an opinionated, stubborn man who doesn't have a clue what he lost when he walked away from me this afternoon. And you're an attorney. I'm not overly fond of attorneys, you know."

"Oh, no?" Nick asked. He tried to rise, but couldn't.

"Sorry, Nick. You're still on the witness stand. Glory's answered her question, now it's your turn. What is your real dream? That inner-secret you've hidden so deep that you won't even visit it while you sleep?"

The entire courtroom was watching him. Nick could feel a sheen of sweat cover his forehead. A man shouldn't sweat in his dreams.

"But we've all agreed this isn't your dream," Fern said.

"No, it's my nightmare," Nick grumbled.

"And Lola isn't your dream," Fern declared.

She didn't seem to realize she didn't need to drive that particular point home. Nick had never fooled himself into thinking that Lola was anything more than a young man's fantasy. She was just a convenient substitute for what Nick really wanted.

"What is your dream, Nick?" Glory repeated her question. "What do you want?"

"I want what Max and Joy and my parents have," Nick admitted.

"What's that?" Bernie pressed.

"I want that kind of love." He stopped and looked at the fiery redhead in front of him. "I want Glory."

"Done," came four fairy voices. Slowly the courtroom faded away, along with everyone in it. Nick sat up in his bed—his cold, lonely bed.

He wanted Glory Chambers. She was his dream come true. "I love Glory," he said out loud. The words swelled his heart. He loved Glory Chambers!

It was a miracle. It was magic. Loving Glory was everything he'd ever dreamed of, and more. He had wished for what his mother and father, and Max and Grace, and Joy and Gabriel shared, and somehow, it had happened. He'd found a woman he could love for the rest of his life.

Now all he had to do was convince her that she loved him, too.

***

Glory glanced at the clock. Four-thirty in the morning? Who the hell would be knocking at her door at four-thirty in the morning?

Her first thought was the fairies. They'd think nothing of waking her from a wonderful dream. A dream that included Nick doing all the wonderful things he'd done to her last night, and more. In her dreams he'd fallen to his knees and said, "I love—"

That's all the further he'd gotten before the knocking on her door had awakened her.

"Damn it," she muttered. She'd never know if her dream-Nick loved her, or if he'd been about to tell her he loved asparagus, or worse yet, brussel sprouts. Who in their right mind could love brussel sprouts?

"Coming," she shouted as she pulled on her decrepit old flannel robe. "Hold your horses."

"Hold yours, Glory, honey," Fern said. "You're not answering the door looking like that."

"Damn it. I admitted I believed you were fairies, but I didn't say you could just pop in on me whenever you wanted." If believing in fairies didn't make her crazy, then having them pop in and out of her room soon would.

"But honey," said Blossom. "If we hadn't popped in you might have answered the door looking like—"

"Like what?" Glory asked, visions of skewered fairies dancing in her head.

"Like *that.* "Fern's exasperation with —that was obvious in her voice.

"Myrtle, would you hurry up!" Blossom hollered.

"Coming." The red-haired fairy popped into the bedroom. And the thumping on the door grew louder.

"Coming!" Glory yelled. "I don't know what's going on, but I want to go back to bed, so the three of you have to clear out."

"Oh, we'll clear out as soon as we take care of you." Blossom's smile said that whatever they were planning didn't bode well for Glory.

"What do you mean, take care?"

"This." A wand appeared in Myrtle's hand, and she waved it.

"This?" Glory asked.

"Look down," Myrtle said.

Glory was no longer wearing her cut off sweats and Temple t-shirt. She was wearing a gossamer pale peach peignoir set. She reached up, and her red curls were no longer bed-head-smooshed, but perfectly styled.

"No morning breath even," Blossom said with a grin. "You're ready to open the door now."

"What's going on?" she asked, more than suspicious.

"Oh, we made a late night call on Glinda. She made Grace's dress for the ball. Did we ever tell you that? Well, we knew right away you needed something special for tonight. So after we left—"

"Left where?" Glory asked.

Blossom ignored her and continued, "—we headed right to Oz. Of course, the Scarecrow asked us to have some tea, but we said no. And you don't know how much I would have enjoyed tea with him because he's a total hunk."

"Blossom, he's stuffed with straw," Fern pointed out.

"And your point is?" Blossom asked, looking annoyed.

There was another loud series of thuds on her door. "Ladies, really I have to get that."

"Oh, yes you do," Blossom gushed. "After all, Glinda worked faster than I've ever seen anyone work to get your outfit done in time. Why she—"

"Blossom, hush. It's time for us to go," Myrtle interrupted. "We'll just show ourselves out. You go get the door." And with that the three fairies disappeared.

"Fairies before coffee is just too much for an ordinary mortal to deal with," Glory muttered as she stormed across her box-cluttered living room. She'd been so busy getting the restaurant opened, and then worrying about fairy trials, she was still practically as packed as the day her moving van had pulled up to the apartment.

Another loud series of thumps hurried her along. “Who is it?” she yelled through the bolted door.

“It’s Nick.” He pounded against the door. “Glory, open up. I’ve got to talk to you.”

“What are the three of you up to?” she whispered to what appeared to be an empty room. It might appear to be empty, but Glory knew better. Those fairies weren’t going anywhere if it meant they might miss something.

“Just open the door, Glory,” Myrtle’s disembodied voice said.

Muttering about fairies and attorneys and coffee, Glory unlatched the door. “What do you want?” she practically growled.

“You.” Nick leaned against the door frame and grinned.

“Me what?”

He pushed past her and waltzed into her apartment, then stood in the center of the living room and turned a full circle. “I love what you’ve done with the place.”

“If you recall, I’ve been a bit busy with the restaurant since I moved. This place just got pushed aside until I had more time. And I repeat, me what? What do you want, Nick.” Coffee. That’s what Glory wanted. Coffee and quiet. No fairies, no crazy attorneys. She wanted time to think.

“No, you want time to talk yourself into hiding away,” she heard Blossom whisper into her ear.

“Get out,” Glory whispered, but apparently not softly enough.

“Nope, I’m not getting out until you understand,” Nick said. He stood right in front of her as he said, “You. I want you.”

“Well, maybe I don’t want you anymore.” Glory tried to sound convincing, but wasn’t quite sure she managed it.

“Yes, you do.” Again that smile, as if Nick had figured out something she hadn’t.

"Of all the egotistical—"

He reached out and traced her forearm with his index finger. Just that one small touch was enough to stop Glory mid-sentence.

"You want me as much as I want you," he said. "The fairies were right. You've been my dream—my secret wish—forever and a day."

"I don't want to want you." That much was the truth. Glory didn't want to want anyone, because wanting led to needing, and if you needed someone they could let you down. She'd been hurt by Garth, and she didn't want to be hurt again.

"I know," he whispered, as if he'd inherited the fairies' ability to read her mind.

"I was married before," she said by way of explanation.

"I know."

"It didn't work out." Despite the fact they'd been together for five years, it wasn't really Cynthia who had broken them up. They'd been broken almost from the beginning. Two strangers sharing a life, but not sharing what really mattered—themselves.

"This will work out," Nick promised.

"How do you know?"

"Because I love you."

"That's what Garth used to say before her found Cynthia and her big boobs." She looked down at the small mounds beneath the gorgeous peignoir. "You're not going to get big with me."

"I saw what you had last night, Glory, and I hope to see them every night for rest of our lives. Besides, more than a handful's just a waste."

She smothered a giggle. "What did you say?" she asked, though she'd heard him the first time.

"More than a handful—"

"No, before that." She wanted to hear him say those

words, those magical words, over and over. They were big, they were scary, and like the fairies had said, they had a magic of their own. He loved her. Nick Aaronson loved Glory Chambers!

It was magic. It was a miracle.

"I want to see you every night for the rest of our lives." His grin said he knew those weren't the words she wanted.

Glory was scared and exhilarated. She was flying higher than any fairy had ever soared. He loved her. She wanted to shout it from the rooftops. "I—" she started.

"Shh," Nick said. "Let me finish, then you can take your turn. I want that happily-ever-after the fairies promised me, and I know that can only happen with you. You're every dream I've ever dreamed. You're the miracle I've been waiting for. I love you."

"You're sure the fairies didn't cast a spell on you?" she teased. But if the fairies had managed to cast a spell on Nick, she'd been caught in it as well.

"They can't make someone love someone. Love is too strong a magic, even for fairies," he said. "No ifs, ands or buts about it. I love you, Glory. I've been waiting my whole life for you, and it took a bunch of fairies to show me that my dream was right in front of me. Do you think you can learn to love me, too?

"Nope."

"Nope?" he echoed in disbelief.

Gently she reached out and caressed his face—the face of the man she wanted to spend the rest of her life waking up to and going to sleep next to. The face of the man she loved. The face of the man who was her happily-ever-after. "I don't have to learn how, because I already love you. I didn't think—didn't dare hope—that you'd feel the same."

"You know, I used to think I'd never find what my family had. I mean, I knew three perfect couples. Their love radiated between them, and it was obvious that each of them was half of a whole. How could I expect to find that? Lightning doesn't strike the same tree four times. And yet, here you are."

Nick looked at the woman he loved and knew he'd found his miracle. He scooped her up. "Tell me that you've at least got a bed in this place?"

"Now that I've got some time, I'm planning to unpack." She pointed toward the bedroom door. "But the bed's set up and it's in there."

"Good. And don't worry about unpacking, at least not until we move these boxes to my house."

"Your house?"

"Unless you want to live somewhere else after we're married."

"Married?" she repeated.

"Sure. You know, my Mom's done nothing but complain about missing Joy and Max's weddings. She's going to badger you into letting her help plan this one." He headed toward the bedroom.

"Wedding?"

"Do you think Bernie would officiate?"

"Wedding?"

Nick set her on the bed. "I know Mom's going to want a huge, blow-out celebration, but she's going to have to plan it fast because I can't wait long. I understand why my siblings didn't wait for a family wedding. I'd whisk you off to Vegas tonight if I didn't know that Mom would kill me." He stripped off his shirt and threw it to the floor. "And though I might have to wait a few weeks for the wedding, I think I'm going to have to insist on jump-starting the honeymoon."

"I think this is one instant I'm in total agreement with you, Counselor."

As he climbed into the bed next to the woman he loved, Nick ran his hand over the silk covering her body. "Have you gotten tired of hearing me say 'I love you?'"

"I'll never get tired of hearing those words." She reached

for him. “I love you, too.”

Nick Aaronson sank into Glory’s glorious embrace and knew he had his miracle.

Epilogue

"And here's a toast to the happy couple," Miriam Aaronson said. "May your life be full of the miracle of love, and may you always find magic in each other's arms."

Three couples burst out laughing, and Miriam looked at her children and their spouses a moment before she added, "And here's to me! I finally got to not only attend, but plan, one of my children's weddings."

Wild applause broke out. They'd rented the Warner Theater. A huge old theater, ornate in the style of an era gone by. The reception took place in its foyer—the perfect setting for the fairy tale wedding Miriam and the fairies had put together in just three weeks.

The fairies had been as insistent on rushing the wedding as Nick. They said they didn't approve of premarital intimate relations, and the sooner they made them legal, the better. But Glory thought they were simply anxious to have things legalized so she and Nick didn't have a chance to change their minds. She could have told them there was no worry. Nick was her dream-come-true.

Glory gazed at her husband. Any place with Nick in it was Fairyland and heaven rolled into one. She looked at her new family. Grace, jiggling CheChe on her knee, was seated next to Joy, who was cuddling a dozing Zeke. Both women were listening to whatever Joy's step-daughter, Sophie, was saying. The little girl had practically stolen the day, bedecked in her flower girl dress.

Max and Gabriel were standing behind the women and children, engaged in some animated discussion. And Miriam, looking smugly at the group, was cuddled on her husband, Joseph's, lap. The love Nick's parents felt for each other and for their family was evident in their indulgent expressions.

"Look at your parents. I hope we feel that strongly about each other thirty or so years down the road," Glory whispered to Nick.

"I have it on good authority that our love will stand the test of time. Hell, if we can survive Myrtle, Fern and Blossom, I can't imagine anything that can tear us apart."

"Where are they, by the way?"

"They're—"

"Right here." Myrtle's dress was as loud as her fire-engine hair, but Glory had become accustomed to Myrtle's flamboyant tastes and thought she looked perfect.

"Thank you, dear," Myrtle said, obviously reading her mind.

Glory was too content to complain.

"We just wanted to stop by and say goodbye," Fern said with a sniff. She smoothed the skirt of her pea-green dress.

"So this is it? You're leaving?" Once upon a time Glory would have said that getting rid of the fairies was her fondest desire. Now she knew she would miss them all fiercely.

"We've got other cases that need our attention." Blossom's gown looked like something Scarlett O'Hara could have worn. Her neon yellow parasol only enhanced the resemblance.

"The restaurant won't be the same without you." That was the truth. Glory would miss her—help.

"I think Dorothy and Don will keep things going well," Myrtle said. "And don't be surprised if they're heating up more than the cooking soon."

"Are you three at it again?" Nick asked.

"Oh, no. Those two didn't need our help," Fern said.

"They just needed the jobs and an introduction."

"Their relationship is a piece of cake. Nothing like trying to fix up the Aaronson clan." Blossom sighed her swoony Southern-belle sigh and twirled her parasol.

"Does Grace have any idea what she's unleashed on the unsuspecting world?" Glory asked with a chuckle.

"Oh, I think she does." Nick squeezed Glory's hand. "And I think the unsuspecting world is a bit better for her unleashing."

"Why thank you, Nick." Fern's voice sounded a little watery, as if she were on the verge of tears. "Fairies don't cry," she said, sounding even closer to tears than before.

"So where are you off to?" Glory asked, hoping to change the subject and avoid fairy tears. If they started crying she knew she would, and crying would ruin her perfect wedding day.

"Well, we're on our way to New York," Blossom said. "Grace's editor is just waiting for her happily-ever-after. She's met us in the books, but has never met us in person."

"Will we see you again?" Nick asked, voicing Glory's unasked question.

Was this what it would be like? Nick reading her mind, Glory reading his. Two halves of a whole?

She thought so.

"Of course," Myrtle whispered.

"Sure you'll see us again," Blossom promised. "Fiona and Bernie want you to come to their wedding."

"They want us to go to Fairyland?" Glory wasn't sure how she felt about that. Fairies in her life was one thing. Going to Fairyland and being surrounded by fairies was another.

"Yes, and you wouldn't believe the fight Bernie had to get you all there." Fern chuckled. "For a stickler for the rules, he's truly loosened up. He and Fiona had a huge argument with the counsel over it. But he won."

"Don't tell him we told," Blossom whispered, glancing across the room. Bernie had officiated over the wedding, and he sat next to Fiona. Their love was evident, even to those without fairy powers. It radiated like an aura, cocooning them. "You should get your invitations any day. See, Fiona got her happily-ever-after, too."

"This isn't goodbye, so no sniffling," Glory said. "You'll get me started, and I'll ruin my make-up."

"Before you go, I'd like to propose a toast." Standing and raising his glass, Nick said, "A toast to Myrtle, Fern and Blossom, three wonderful women who have brought magic and love into our lives."

"Hear, hear," chorused the rest of the wedding party.

For years afterwards, the guests at the wedding argued over what happened next. But it appeared that the three women shrank to the size of someone's forearm and sprouted small wings and blinked out of sight. As they disappeared everyone heard, "And they all lived happily ever after."

Which, of course, they did.

ABOUT THE AUTHOR

Holly Fuhrmann lives in Erie, PA and lives with one husband, four children, and one drooling Old English Mastiff, which makes her a leading authority on sanity-challenged writers. Her fairytale trilogy, Mad About Max, Magic for Joy and Miracles for Nick are currently available through ImaJinn Books.

She loves to hear from her readers. You can visit her at her homepage http://www.HollysBooks.com or write to her at PO Box 11102, Erie, PA 16514-1102.

DON'T MISS
HOLLY FUHRMANN'S

MAD ABOUT MAX

ISBN 1-893896-05-6
(Book One of the Fairy Godmother Trilogy)

MAGIC FOR JOY

ISBN 1-893896-19-6
(Book Two of the Fairy Godmother Trilogy)

For more information about Ms. Ferguson's books, visit our web site at:http://www.imajinnbooks.com